Ten Seconds to Play!
Fourth Down Showdown

Fourth Down Showdown

BOOKS BY

CLAIR BEE

TECHNICAL

Basketball for Everyone
Winning Basketball Plays
The Basketball Coach's Handbook
The Clair Bee Basketball Quiz Book
Basketball for Future All-American Stars
Make the Team in Basketball

The CLAIR BEE *Basketball Library*

The Science of Coaching
Basketball Fundamentals and Techniques
Individual and Team Basketball Drills
Man-to-Man Defense and Attack
Zone Defense and Attack

FICTION

The CHIP HILTON *Stories*

Touchdown Pass
Championship Ball
Strike Three!
Clutch Hitter!
Hoop Crazy
Pitchers' Duel
A Pass and a Prayer
Dugout Jinx
Freshman Quarterback
Backboard Fever
Fence Busters
Ten Seconds to Play!
Fourth Down Showdown
Tournament Crisis
Hardcourt Upset
Pay-Off Pitch
No-Hitter
Triple-Threat Trouble
Backcourt Ace
Buzzer Basket
Comeback Cagers
Home Run Feud
Hungry Hurler

A CHIP HILTON SPORTS STORY

Fourth Down Showdown

BY CLAIR BEE

GROSSET & DUNLAP Publishers New York

PRINTED IN THE UNITED STATES OF AMERICA

To my pal

JIMMY LOWE

Contents

CHAPTER 1

A CALCULATED RISK

CHIP HILTON's long legs easily matched the leisurely trotting strides of Fireball Finley, Speed Morris, and Ace Gibbons as they jogged around the field. But it took all his will power to restrain the impulse to turn the lazy pace into a race. Chip felt like tearing around the cinder track and out the straightaway and right up the wide concrete steps to the top of the stadium wall.

The massive concrete bowl which surrounded the striped football field filled Chip with awe, even though the seats were empty. Come Saturday, there would be fifty thousand fans covering those seats like the frosting on a cake and they would be cheering for the team—and maybe for Chip Hilton. And down in Valley Falls, his mother and all his hometown friends would be watching on television and picking out Soapy and Biggie and Speed and Red and maybe State's new starting quarterback. Chip glanced at the field. "It's beautiful," he murmured, "just like an emerald set in a band of black gold."

As the foursome made the final turn of the track,

Chip could restrain his exuberance no longer. "Come on!" he shouted. "Let's go!"

Chip's backfield teammates accepted the challenge with joyous shouts and spurted for the lead. Chip churned the cinders for a few steps and then lengthened his stride. By that time he was well out in front. Behind him, he heard the pounding cleats of his pursuers and then he really turned on the steam, gradually pulling away. He flashed into the concrete tunnel leading to the dressing room and up the steps to the door before he slowed down. Breathing easily, he turned just in time to escape a good-natured swipe from Speed Morris' flailing arm.

"You got the jump!" Speed reminded his high-school pal. He took a deep breath. "Good thing for you," he blustered. "Next time I'll be out in front!"

"Oh, sure!" Fireball Finley grunted, slamming on the brakes and banging into the door. "What makes you think you can run?"

Ace Gibbons eased his heavy frame to a stop. "He's a scatback," he gibed. "Didn't you know?"

Morris ignored the late arrivals and laughed derisively. "Everything's all right now, Chip," he said, nodding toward Ace and Fireball. "The tanks have finally arrived."

The fleet runner was saved from the good-natured violence of Ace and Fireball by the appearance of the rest of State's varsity and snickered gleefully as he darted through the door.

Curly Ralston's "three laps and in" didn't mean that State's varsity was through for the day. Far from it! Ralston always scheduled a skull session to follow the workouts and he was waiting in the "skull room" when they finished with the showers. He went right to work on the blackboard, drawing in the plays and shooting questions at one player and another until he had covered every person on the squad. "Nice going," he said, at last. "We've been through this time and again, men, but it's impossible to develop coordination and timing in a new system without hours and hours of practice and study. It takes some teams two and often three years to change over, but you've made the change in a matter of weeks—" The determined lips slackened again. "That's the reason," he continued pointedly, "that Coach Rockwell and Jim Sullivan and I are convinced that you have the makings of a great team. Not next year or the year after—but this year!

Sophomores or not! Now, get a good night's rest. You looked good today. Real good."

When Ralston finished, Chip hustled for the door. Fireball Finley, Philip Whittemore, and Soapy Smith were right on his heels.

"Late again!" Soapy exploded. "That guy's gonna keep workin' us late every night and we're gonna be lookin' for new jobs."

"Say that again!" Whittemore agreed. "George Grayson sure must love football to put up with us."

"Maybe," Chip said. "Maybe he just likes to help fellows work their way through school."

"Well," Fireball said gratefully, "whatever it is, we're lucky."

Whittemore sighed deeply. "I wish this night was over," he said. "We're going to be mobbed. I wish Grayson would give us some more help on the fountain."

"Chip's the one who needs help," Soapy protested. "He never catches up. Syrups for the fountain, toothpaste and combs for the cosmetics counter, change for Mitzi, perfumes for Mary Hill, pocketbooks, alarm clocks, light bulbs, lipstick, hot-water bottles, back scratchers, candy, pencils, pens, baby diapers, toys—"

Fireball groaned. "Please!" he protested. "I'm tired just listening."

Whittemore was right. State Drug was jammed when they arrived and it was mobbed the rest of the evening. Soapy, Fireball, and Whitty dished out cokes, frosteds, sundaes, malteds, and banana splits until they were dizzy.

Chip was on the run all evening, too. Keeping up with the stockroom demands of a big outfit like State Drug was no joke. His first chance for a rest came about ten o'clock and he sank down on the chair by the desk with a sigh of relief. A few seconds later he heard the door open but he was too tired to lift his head.

"Excuse me, Chip."

Chip leaped to his feet in confusion, the blood rushing to his face. "Gosh, Mr. Grayson! I—I'm sorry!"

"That's all right, Chip. Sit down. I've been checking up on your job and I'm convinced that you need help. I guess you'll be glad to know that I've been running an ad in the paper for a youngster to help you out evenings and Saturdays."

Chip started to protest but Mr. Grayson checked him. "Now, Chip, I know this store and I believe I could write a pretty fair job description for every person on the payroll. You need help, period! O.K.?"

Chip nodded. "If you say so, Mr. Grayson. But it doesn't seem right, letting me off for practice and games and then getting someone to help me do my work. I—"

"Have I ever complained, Chip?"

"No, sir. But—"

Mr. Grayson checked him. "Suppose we forget it. Now, about the boy. The working age is fifteen and there will be a lot of applicants to see you tomorrow night. Choose a boy who *needs* the job. One you like. Don't forget that he must have working papers. Oh, by the way, I'm putting on a couple of extra soda clerks evenings and Saturdays, too. And, Chip . . .

"I realize what a tough battle you and Soapy and Whittemore and Finley are putting up. And I'd be greatly disappointed if you fellows didn't prove to yourselves and to a lot of other youngsters that a fellow can take part in sports and work his way through school and still keep up with his studies. Good night, son."

After Mr. Grayson left, Chip tried his hand at writing a job description for his stockroom assistant. As he wrote, he pictured the boy he would like to help. The selection was important to the job but it was important to him as well. Chip wanted to give the job to a boy who helped out at home. The difficult time his mother had endured following the death of his father had imbued in Chip an intense desire to help other unfortunate families.

STOCKROOM ASSISTANT DUTIES AND RESPONSIBILITIES

GENERAL PROCEDURE: The stockroom contains many valuable items. The receipt, sorting, storing, replacement, care, and issue to the proper department is the responsibility of the stockroom clerk and his assistant. It is important that every item be stored in its proper place so that quantities on hand may be quickly checked and requisitions promptly filled.

The key to the stockroom is to be obtained from the cashier, Miss Mitzi Savrill, each afternoon when you report for work, and turned over to the stockroom clerk when he arrives. The door is to be locked and the key given to Miss Savrill for safekeeping if you are sent out of the store on an errand.

All items and material issued from the stockroom must be entered on a stockroom requisition receipt and this form must be initialed by the stockroom clerk. It must be checked and signed by the department head when delivery is made. Do not leave the respective department until the requisition receipt is signed.

DUTIES IN THE ORDER OF PERFORMANCE

1. Collect requisitions from each department and place on stick file on stockroom desk.

2. Fill all syrup containers and return them to the fountain. (Containers must be sterilized by lunch counter supervisor.)
3. Open incoming deliveries and sort carefully so storeroom clerk can check each item against purchase order.
4. Clean and dust stockroom carefully. Replace all stock on proper shelves.
5. Make deliveries to department supervisors.

"That's it," Chip murmured when he finished. "Now for a good night's rest."

The following evening, Soapy exploded into the stockroom and into Chip's thoughts with his usual abruptness. "Big crowd of kids outside, Chip. Just like a Saturday morning movie. Funny thing, though. Only two came in. I'll send 'em in to see you one at a time, O.K.?"

The first applicant's physical qualifications were favorable. The boy was well built, about five feet, four inches in height, Chip judged, and weighed about one hundred and forty pounds. But the boy was arrogant in his bearing and almost antagonistic in his attitude. His keen black eyes swept swiftly around the room and back to Chip.

"What's the job pay?" he demanded.

Chip hoped his smile was friendly. "Let's talk a little about you, first," he suggested gently. "What's your name?"

"Tony! Tony Carlara!"

"What does your father do, Tony?"

"He works! What d'ya think?"

"What kind of work does he do?"

"Anything he can get. He's a laborer."

"Do you have any brothers or sisters?"

"In our family? That's a laugh! We're a big family."

"Just how important *is* this job to your family, Tony?"

"The family! What they got to do with it? I'm my own boss! What I earn, I keep!"

"Don't you help out at home?"

"Me help out? What for? Why should I? That's the old man's responsibility. I got my own problems."

Chip questioned Tony a little longer and then wrote his address on an application blank. "I'll let you know, Tony," he said kindly.

Tony's intelligent eyes probed Chip's gray eyes and held steady. "Who you kiddin'!" he said belligerently. "You ain't gonna hire me." He swaggered to the door and paused with his hand on the knob. "See you around," he said contemptuously. Then he slammed the door, leaving Chip bewildered.

The second applicant was taller and heavier than Carlara but just as arrogant. So the interview didn't last long. Just long enough for Chip to learn that the boy's name was Bucky Husta and that he was Tony Carlara's pal. After Husta left, Chip waited uncertainly for the next applicant. "Maybe I don't know how to talk to boys who are looking for a job," he mused. "Something's wrong."

Much to his surprise, there were no more applicants. And when he and Soapy and Fireball and Whitty started for home the crowd of boys had disappeared with the exception of Tony Carlara and Bucky Husta. They were lounging just outside the main entrance. Chip started to speak, but they avoided his eyes and sauntered slowly away.

"That's funny," Chip said.

"What's funny?" Soapy demanded.

"The other kids. Why in the world didn't any of the other kids apply for the job?"

"Got me," Soapy said. "Heck with it! C'mon! We only got ten minutes to get home. Ralston's probably got detectives watchin' us right now to see that we're home before eleven o'clock."

CHAPTER 2

SHOULDER TO SHOULDER

PETE RANDOLPH was the most ingenious building superintendent on State's campus. He had installed a system of bells in the Jefferson dormitory which announced every hour on the hour throughout the day beginning at seven o'clock in the morning. Many and devious were the methods used by Jeff's residents to "beat the system." Jump wiring, short-circuit fuses, and bent bell-hammers had given respite to the inventors on many occasions. The clanging of the bells meant little or nothing to Chip and his pals. Since all were working at one job or another to help defray their college expenses, they had decided before school opened to set aside two hours for group study every morning. And that meant early rising. No one was excused unless he had a class or the meeting interfered with his job.

Soapy Smith had long ago arbitrarily appointed himself "rabble rouser" for his second-floor pals and he never failed. Every morning, Saturday, Sunday, holiday, or schoolday, Soapy rapped on each door at seven o'clock. This particular morning, he herded his charges out of bed and over to the cafeteria and then startled his listeners by stating abruptly, "I've been thinkin'!"

"Wonders never cease," Fireball observed in an awed voice.

Soapy fixed a baleful eye on Finley, took another sip of milk, and continued, "Chip and I were talking about Mr. Grayson last night after we went to bed and I figure we ought to do something to show him our appreciation. Chip and I have worked for him for a year now, and he's been swell. Lets us off for practices and every time there's a game he hires substitutes for us and pays us just the same. He's the nicest man I ever met." Soapy thought that over a second and then added, "Next to Rock."

"I think so too, Soapy," Finley said softly. "What's on your mind?"

"Well," Soapy continued, "I've been thinkin' that maybe we could skip our lunch and supper time and come in earlier on Saturdays and work a little harder . . ." He hesitated and then continued, "Chip's just got to have someone to help him in the stockroom, but I think we can get along without any more help on the fountain if we *really* put out."

"I'm game for that," Whittemore said, nodding approvingly. "I know I could work a lot faster."

There was a deep, reflective silence as they thought over Soapy's suggestion. Whittemore and Finley had not known Soapy very long, and they must have found this sudden reversal confusing. To them, he probably was just the funster. Except on the football field, of course.

Chip had been a silent observer. Now he took part in the discussion. "Someone should tell Mr. Grayson," he suggested.

"Soapy's idea, Soapy's job," Finley said decisively. "Come on. Let's hit the books!"

"Just a sec," Soapy remonstrated. "Let me finish these eggs. Costs money, you know."

"By the way," Whittemore drawled, while they waited. "How come you don't get Biggie up in the mornings? He too tough? Or does he have some kind of a drag?"

"Yeah," Finley chimed in. "He sleeps more than any six men I ever saw. In bed at nine every night and every minute of the day except when he has classes. Must have sleeping sickness!"

Soapy looked at Chip. "You tell 'em," he said.

"There isn't much to tell," Chip said simply. "Biggie is working his way through school just like we are. Only he's got a tougher job. He works nights."

"Nights?" Finley echoed. "Doing what?"

"You ever been down in the boiler room after midnight?" Chip countered. Finley shook his head and Chip continued, "Well, if you ever find it necessary, you'll find Biggie in charge of the boiler. Every night from twelve o'clock until six in the morning."

"Ralston know that?" Whittemore asked.

"Don't think so," Chip said softly. "Biggie doesn't talk much about himself."

"C'mon, you guys," Soapy said, rising and gulping down the rest of his milk. "I've got to get busy on psychology. Prof Engels is my pal. Gonna give me an A come February, I hope, I hope!"

It required all of Chip's powers of concentration to stay on the ball and absorb the lectures of his professors that day. Soapy's attitude regarding George Grayson had struck a deep chord and Chip couldn't get the responsibilities of his job out of his mind. Mr. Grayson was a strict disciplinarian, but he had earned the loyalty of his employees because of his kindness and understanding. Chip had always gone all-out in his desire to operate the stockroom with efficiency and now he realized that continued success depended on his selection of a good helper. The behavior of the two applicants the previous evening and the failure of the other boys to apply for the job had him stumped. He was glad when his last class was finished.

Football was different. A fellow could run and block and kick and pass and get rid of his excess steam in a hundred different ways. He hurried down to the gym and into his practice uniform and hustled out on the field. Once there, he forgot all about State Drug and George Grayson and lectures, and concentrated on the job of holding his postition as State's Number One quarterback. And that took some doing, because his chief rival was the veteran regular, Tims Lansing.

Ralston had shocked more than one loyal State fan when he had broken up a veteran team and inserted a number of sophomore hopefuls in the starting line-up for the opening game against Tech. And he had surprised everyone, including the members of his coaching staff, when he had discarded his famous straight T attack in favor of the unbalanced split-T.

The seriousness of this last scrimmage before the Brandon game hit Chip with the impetus of one of Biggie's tackles. It was obvious in the serious faces of the displaced veterans and in the studied nonchalance of the sophomores who had looked so good in the Tech game.

Sullivan put them through a fast grass drill and followed with a series of wind sprints. Then he brought them in on a run to circle Curly Ralston.

"Men," Ralston said, "this will be our last contact workout before the Brandon game. We'll run our plays slow motion, first, and then at game speed. I'd like to go through the basic series before Nibs Nelson brings his frosh team over here to demonstrate Brandon's single wing."

The Valley Falls contingent never planned their moves, but at times of importance they could always be found shoulder to shoulder. Chip glanced at his pals. Soapy, Biggie, Red, and Speed were standing quietly beside him and, flanking them, were two newcomers. Fireball Finley and Philip Whittemore had moved so unobtrusively into the little circle that each was accepted now without a single reservation. Not a word was spoken, but all were gripped by the same thought, "A good showing this afternoon means a starting berth against Brandon on Saturday."

"Red shirts for Team A, Murph," Ralston continued. "Blue for Team B. Rock, you take Team A; I'll handle Team B—

"Team A line: Whittemore, Higgins, Cohen, Maxim, McCarthy, Smith, and Brennan. Team B line: Curtis, Schwartz, Morgan, Carlson, Anderson, Clark, and Leopoulos.

"Team A backs: Hilton, Finley, Morris, and Gibbons! Team B: Lansing, Roberts, Cole, and Burk!"

It was a hard, bruising workout. Much worse than actual scrimmage. Ralston stood behind Team A and gave the signal for the play he wanted Team B to run. On the opposite side of the line, Rockwell did the same. But no matter how cleverly the coaches attempted to conceal the play, the players knew what was coming. That made for head-to-head man-slaughter.

Chip was playing in the safety position and didn't get in the actual contact work except when his team ran the ball. But he was glad when Nibs Nelson appeared with his frosh team. Not that it made much difference. The big varsity line smothered the frosh interpretation of Brandon's single wing. And on the offense, the varsity attack was too strong. Ralston called off the scrimmage after thirty minutes of futile work.

After the showers the squad assembled in the skull room and Ralston went right to work. "I wasn't impressed with our offensive blocking this afternoon," he said sharply. "Frankly, I'm not sure we're all trying to do the same thing.

"It's important that you remember that no matter how opponents change their defensive alignments, it is impossible for them to change our unbalanced line positions. That is the reason we have indicated the holes between our own linemen as the points of attack rather than defensive opponents. Simplified, it means that every player on our team knows exactly *where* we are trying to clear a path, irrespective of the moves of opponents. Are there any questions?"

Tiny Tim McCarthy raised his hand. "Coach," he said, "I'm not clear on what to do when an opponent submarines. It's almost impossible to move him out of the hole."

"You're right, Tim," Ralston agreed. "So, do it the easy way. Fall on him and duck. That will clear the hole and the back can go right on over the top and through the hole."

"Need a power shovel to dig the guy out," Soapy whispered hoarsely.

The whisper brought smiles but no laughs. Ralston didn't go for levity where football was concerned. He glanced sharply in Soapy's direction and continued.

"Now, I'm going to call a name and the number of a play and I want the player named to call out as quickly as possible who carries the ball and where. O.K.? All right, Lansing: Thirteen!"

Lansing's reply was quick and precise. "Right halfback between right guard and right tackle."

"Brennan: Forty!"

"Quarterback to the right of the center, Coach."

"Cohen: Twenty-six!"

"Fullback tight to the outside of left end."

"Maxim: Three-five!"

It was a cross-up in the method of calling the play but it meant the same thing. Maxim reacted promptly. "Left halfback off right tackle!"

"Whittemore: Forty-eight!"

"Hil—" Whittemore caught himself. "Quarterback wide around left end, Coach."

There was a pause and it was clear that State's varsity had devoted a lot of time to learning their plays. Ralston nodded approvingly. "Nice going, men. Now, one more thing. Sullivan has diagramed some of our basic plays. I'm sure you can determine the proper signals. Coach Sullivan will hand them to you on your way out. That's all."

Soapy was the first person out the door. He grabbed the sheet of paper from Sullivan and waited impatiently for his State Drug buddies. "C'mon," he urged impatiently. "It's five minutes to six. We're gonna have to run to make it. Besides, I gotta tell Mr. Grayson we can handle the fountain without any more help."

Chip took the lead and set a fast pace, but it was five minutes after six when they reached the store. And there, just outside the main entrance, Chip was surprised to see Tony Carlara and Bucky Husta. The two boys were apparently engrossed in the window display, but when Chip halted, they walked quickly away.

"Well, what d'ya know?" Soapy said. "Your pals are back."

During the long, busy evening, Soapy managed to get back to the stockroom to report on his talk with Mr. Grayson and on the presence of Tony Carlara and Bucky Husta. Chip went outside several times to question the two youngsters, but by the time he reached the door, they had disappeared.

It was the same Friday night and Saturday morning. Tony and Bucky were right on the job, but not a single other applicant showed up. Chip tried in vain to catch the two boys and would have regarded the strange game as good fun except for his urgent need for help.

"I'll settle this tonight," he assured his pals when they started for the stadium. "If I have to chase those kids all the way to Valley Falls!"

CHAPTER 3

STARTING QUARTERBACK

CHIP was the first man suited up. He tried to concentrate on his uniform, fussing with the sleeves of his jersey and his shoulder pads. Then he tried on his headgear and adjusted the chin strap. Next, he unlaced his right shoe, took it off, carefully inspected the kicking toe, and laced it on again. All the time, he was conscious of the old familiar knot in his stomach and the tight feeling in his chest. But Chip wasn't the only player in the room who was having suit-up trouble. Most of the sophomores were experiencing the same difficulty.

Murph Kelly, State's wise old trainer, recognized the signs and began chattering away. "We're breaking a three-year jinx this afternoon, gang. Mark my words! We've lost the second game on our schedule for the last three years and we're changing that this afternoon!

"Come on, Smith! Turn that pad around and lace it up in front. What d'ya think it is, a corset?

"Oh, no, you don't, McCarthy. Take off that sock and get those ankles taped. Every man tapes his ankles for scrimmages and games. You know that! Besides, it's Coach's orders!"

Hours later, it seemed to Chip, he found himself on the field. A quick glance showed that the stadium was packed clear up to the rim. Then the warm-up drills and the kicking and the passing was over and he was standing in front of the bench with the starters, champing his cleats on the grass and trying to listen to Ralston's last-second instructions. Captain Mike Brennan charged into the circle, pulling on his headgear, and rasping, "We kick! We kick!" and Chip trotted out on the field while the State fans rose as one man and cheered the appearance of the team.

Back in position for the kick-off, Chip tried to concentrate on the ball. But it was swaying from side to side on the kicking T and his legs felt as though they were made of soda straws. Then a whistle shrilled and Chip raised his arms and stretched them wide as he lurched toward the ball. At that precise instant, sudden strength and power flooded him, and the ball steadied and looked as big as a pumpkin. Chip drove forward, figuring he could kick a hole in the ball and he tried to do just that.

It was a good kick, angled toward the right, and it carried to the goal line. Brandon demonstrated right then and there that State was in for a busy afternoon. The five tall, rangy forwards sped back across the restraining line and formed in front of the receiver almost as soon as he caught the ball. The ball carrier picked up the wedge and kept in its shelter as far as the thirty. There, he broke out to his right and angled for the side line.

Cohen broke the wedge on his side and Whittemore should have made the tackle. But Whitty overshot the mark and the runner slipped past him and darted past the forty-yard line—away, it seemed, for a sure touchdown. Chip had followed the ball and was caught on the wrong side of the wedge. But Speed Morris, playing safety on the kick-off, took care of the desperate situation, cutting the runner down on the mid-field stripe with a beautiful driving tackle which brought a roar of relief from the home stands.

Brennan immediately yelled for a time-out and called his team into the huddle. "Forget it, gang," he said crisply. "Settle down, now. It won't happen again! Remember what Sullivan said about their passing. They'll open up now! Try for a quick score!"

When play was resumed, Brandon's left halfback faked a pass downfield and then threw a hard, fast peg to his quarterback in the right flat. Fireball had followed the receiver out in the flat and gambled on an interception. But he was a step too slow and the speedy field general gathered in the ball and cut laterally toward the left. It was amazing how quickly his downfield blockers formed.

Brennan, backing up the other side of the line, came across fast, but he met the full impact of the blockers and didn't have a chance. Chip had picked up the Brandon left end who had outdistanced Gibbons, and Ace turned back just in time to bring the runner down on the thirty-yard line.

Brennan called for the 5-3-3 defense in the huddle and Chip hurried back to the twenty-yard line. Chip was now gravely aware that Brandon was a top-flight aggregation with a fast and determined line and a lightning-fast backfield. The visitors cross-bucked for six, reversed inside Higgins for five more, and it was first and ten on the State nineteen-yard line. The Brandon fullback hit the strong side tackle for three and came right back up the middle for five more. An end-around play carried to the State five-yard line, and it was first down and goal to go. Brennan took another time-out.

Ralston sent Schwartz in for Higgins, Curtis for Whittemore, and Cole for Morris, while the "hold-that-line" chant of the home fans boomed across the field. The chant became a roar and Chip could scarcely hear the Brandon quarterback calling his signals. Then the eagle-eyed passer spotted his lanky right end leading Boots Cole toward the right corner of the end zone and rifled a finger-tip pass over Cole's head. It was a touchdown! The speedy Brandon fullback booted a perfect placement to make the score: Brandon 7, State 0.

State's fans had the right idea and expressed it. "We want a touchdown! We want a touchdown!"

Chip's favorite play was the runback of a punt or a kick-off. It gave him the same thrill that he experienced in baseball when he got hold of one and sent it winging over the fence for a home run. "Now's the time," he told himself.

The thump was clear and piercing and the ball came spinning high in the air and right at Chip. He had to wait for the ball on the five-yard line and the fleet Brandon tacklers were at the fifteen when he gathered it in. The State wedge was far ahead and Chip had only the blocking of Fireball, Boots Cole, and Ace Gibbons to meet the swarm of tacklers. They weren't enough and he was buried on the twelve-yard line under a pile of eager visitors.

Chip was shaken up on the play but he leaped

swiftly to his feet and hurried back to the huddle. "All right, gang," he said sharply. "Twenty-one on four! Hip!"

Up to the line and, on the fourth number, Brennan gave Chip the ball with the sharp plunk which always filled him with confidence. He pivoted to his left, faked a hand-off to Cole with his right hand, and, holding the ball behind his back with his left hand, slipped it to Fireball. It was clever hidden-ball stuff and Fireball exploded into the line and out and up to the twenty before he was brought down. State's fans roared approval of that bit of sleight-of-hand and it gave Chip a big lift. He came right back with another straightaway play.

"One-four on three, gang!" Chip said, winking at Ace Gibbons. "Give us some help, Biggie, Wally! Hip!"

Ace Gibbons was hard and fast and he hit behind the blocking of Cohen and Curtis like a mad bull. His plunge was good for six yards and a first down. Chip kept alternating Fireball and Gibbons, and as they ripped off gain after gain and first down after first down, his confidence returned.

Then disaster struck. Chip sent Boots Cole over right tackle after faking to Gibbons. Boots made the difficult up-and-back stride and dashed between Maxim and Schwartz at a mile-a-minute clip but fumbled the ball. Brandon recovered on its own twenty-five.

It was hard to take, but Chip pulled Cole to his feet and whacked him on the back. "My fault, Boots," he said. "It was a bad pass."

"Come on, gang!" Brennan urged. "We'll get it back!"

State had the determination and fought tooth and

nail. But Brandon controlled the ball, stopped State's running attack cold, and drove relentlessly into State territory time after time. Chip's kicking was magnificent but the visitors kept knocking at the door and finally broke through for their second touchdown. The score at the half was: Brandon 14, State 0.

In the dressing room, Chip leaned forward and dug his fingernails deep in the edge of the wooden bench on which he sat. His immobility and intent gaze seemed to indicate that he was tired out, that he was giving his arms and legs and muscles a much-needed rest. But the rigid position of his body testified otherwise.

Inwardly, Chip was tearing himself apart. His first-half performance had been atrocious. It had been foolish to rest on the laurels he had earned the previous week, he told himself. One game didn't make a season. Instead of playing his own game and mixing up his plays and forgetting everything except the winning of the game, he had tried to make each of his backfield teammates look good and had forgotten all about himself.

Ralston believed in giving his quarterbacks a free rein. He schooled them in his type of attack in the practice workouts and skull sessions and let them do their own field-generaling in the games. Chip had appreciated the freedom but he was far from happy with his selection of the plays for that first half. He had fallen for Fireball's exuberant confidence and had used the blockbuster too often. It had been the same with Ace Gibbons. As the only veteran in the starting backfield, Ace was entitled to every consideration, but Chip had leaned over backward. Now he was paying for his weakness.

Yes, that's what it was, he thought. Weakness!

A quarterback's job was to pilot his team to victory and it was of little importance who carried the ball, made the touchdowns, or got the cheers.

Ralston's cool, penetrating voice broke into Chip's thoughts. "All right, men. Give me your attention."

The piece of chalk, incongruously fragile in the broad hand of the coach, glided across the board. "Whittemore! Back in at end!"

Chip's eyes flickered toward Whitty. The big junior college graduate had really come into his own in the Tech game. Whitty had won the all-important opening game almost by himself. With ten seconds left to play, Whitty had faked a block and then reversed around behind Chip on a modern version of the old, time-worn Statue of Liberty play. It was good for a touchdown and the victory. Whitty belonged! He was six-four, weighed two hundred and ten pounds, and he could move his rangy frame like a scatback. Wally Curtis was an experienced senior and almost as big, but Whittemore was better by far. . . .

"—Cohen! Rush the passer! We didn't get across the line fast enough nor far enough in the first half."

Chip followed Ralston's glance. Biggie Cohen was six-four, two hundred and forty pounds of steel, and as quick as a tiger. Troubles Morgan was as tall but fifty pounds lighter. The veteran was good but he couldn't play left tackle like Biggie. Nobody, but nobody, on this team or any other, could measure up to Biggie. Chip glanced at his home-town pal again. Biggie hadn't moved a muscle.

"—Anderson! You're fast enough and small enough to slip through those holes in the Brandon line. I want to see you in Brandon's backfield on every play!"

Chip liked Eddie. The sophomore guard was five-nine and weighed only one hundred and eighty-five pounds but he was a whale of a scrapper. Fast, too! But Tiny Tim McCarthy weighed two hundred and forty five pounds and was as fast. On the defense, Tiny Tim was the best middle guard Chip had ever seen.

"—Brennan! Strengthen our pass defense. They're passing us silly!"

Chip evaluated State's rugged captain. Mike was an even six feet in height and weighed two hundred and five pounds. He was a member of the junior class, but when it came to football, Mike was a Ph.D. Chip's eyes flashed toward Bebop Leopoulos. Bebop was as big as Brennan but there the comparison ended. Mike Brennan was a hustling, fighting leader, an expert center, and a raging lion on the defense. Mike was a cinch for All-Conference, maybe All-America. . . .

Ralston's voice bit through again. "Clark! You heard what I told Anderson. Same goes for you! Except when you're playing in the secondary against passes. Then I want to see you cover the hole down the middle like a blanket."

Chip didn't agree on that selection. Ralston knew best, of course. But when it came to pass defense and all-round guard play, Soapy was the greatest. Clark had been through the mill, but Soapy had a nose for interceptions and he was bigger and tougher.

"—Maxim! Crash a little more, Joe. Ride that big end a bit on your way after the passer. He's their best receiver."

Chip agreed on that selection, all right. Who wouldn't! Silent Joe was only a sophomore but he had nailed down the right-tackle spot from the very first day of practice. Joe was six-two, one hundred and ninety-five pounds, and a deadly blocker and tackler. He never gave his opponent a second of rest on the offense or defense. Joe was good enough for any man's team. . . .

"—Higgins! I want you to crash, too! Use your height to knock the ball down the passer's throat!"

Larry Higgins reminded Chip of Sky Bollinger, State's freshman basketball center. Larry was a six-five, one-hundred-and-eighty-pound "shadow" who was almost as good as Whittemore when it came to pulling in the passes. "He'll be all over the Brandon passer this half," Chip breathed to himself.

Time was running out and Ralston's words came faster and faster. "—Cole! Gibbons! Finley! Lansing! I want to see every receiver covered on every play. Check with one another and then check again. Don't fall for the fake line-bucks and slants. Watch the ends. If they come out of the line fast and head up-field, it means business. Don't let anyone get behind you. Understand?

"All right, now, let's sum it up! Good defense. A fast hard-charging line deep in the Brandon back-field. Smart covering of pass receivers! Mike! Use a five-man line when you smell a pass situation. Try the umbrella pass defense! And check coverage of every receiver—

"Now the offense! Lansing! Mix up your attack! Don't gamble. We've got lots of time. Thirty long minutes. Open 'em up with passes and then strike on the ground. When they tighten up the line, hit through the air!

"Mike, it's our choice. Better receive! We need the ball! All right, men. Let's go!"

Chip didn't have much time to think about Ralston's second-half backfield right then, because every player in the room surged around Ralston in an attempt to join in the team clasp. But, mobbed and pushed as he was, he didn't forget that he had lost out as State's starting quarterback.

CHAPTER 4

A LESSON IN STRATEGY

STATE is a big-little university. Students never get "lost" on the campus or in the classroom, and the professors make it a point to know their students. The sports fans are like that, too. They are with you —win, lose, or draw! Now, they rose to their feet en masse and expressed their loyalty with a cheer which exploded like a bomb and held its volume until the kick-off.

Chip headed for a blanket and a seat on the bench and then allowed himself to think about the second-half backfield. He started with Tims Lansing, State's veteran quarterback. Lansing was about his own height and weight, six-two and one hundred and eighty-five pounds, give or take a little, but Tims was four years older and had two years of big-time football experience under his belt. Chip knew that he was a better passer, kicker, and runner than Lansing. But he knew, too, that a quarterback had to have a lot more than just football skills.

"It's my own fault," Chip whispered under his breath. "Why in the world did I let sentiment influence my judgment? The coach gave me my chance and I fluffed out. Before fifty thousand people! A fine time to freeze up! I'd better concentrate on Lansing and learn something about field generalship. . . ."

Soapy was disgusted. He threw the blanket up over his head and peered angrily out at everyone in sight. Then he jabbed a heavy elbow in Chip's ribs. "Don't be a chump, Chip," he growled reproachfully. "This is for keeps! Carry the ball yourself once in a while. And pass and kick the way you should. Forget those other guys! O.K.?"

Chip nodded grimly. "Don't worry," he promised. "I'll never make *that* mistake again. That is, if I get another chance."

"You'll get another chance," Soapy muttered. "Don't fluff it!"

State was out on the field, now, and Chip scanned the other backs. He'd sure go along with Ralston when it came to Fireball. The big fullback was the hardest running back Chip had ever seen. Finley could break through a hole in the line and be out in the open before you knew he had the ball. Furthermore, Fireball was six feet in height and weighed two hundred and ten pounds, all steel muscle. He was almost as durable as State's concrete stadium.

Gibbons at right halfback could have come out of the same mold. Ace had been State's regular fullback the year before but he had been shifted to right halfback to make room for Finley.

"We've sure got 'em," Chip breathed, thinking of Lou Little's formula for a winning college team. "Two big tackles and a fullback!"

Soapy's head swung around. "What did you say?" he demanded.

Chip shook his head. "Nothing, Soapy. Just thinking out loud." He focused his eyes on Boots Cole. Boots was a senior, five-eleven in height and weighed one hundred and sixty-five pounds. He was a good, steady halfback. But Chip preferred his high school teammate, Speed Morris. Speed was about the same size at five-eleven and one hundred and seventy pounds, but he was a streak of lightning with the ball. Once past the line, Speed had what it took to go all the way. He had swivel hips and a change of pace which had bewildered many a cocksure tackler.

Chip found himself on his feet, then, the blanket tumbling unnoticed to the ground, as he joined the bench warmers in cheering the players on the field. The crowd noise was deafening as Brandon's wave of gold-and-black-clad players started slowly and then surged down the field in fleet pursuit of the spinning ball. The second half was on!

It was a fairly short boot and Fireball took the ball on the dead run. Heading straight up the middle, the blockbuster sprinted past his own blockers and burst through the tip of the wedge and out in the open. Fireball's speed was so blinding that one tackler, then another, and finally two more went spinning off his pounding knees. Then the kicker missed him completely and it looked like he might get clear away. But the Brandon safety saved the day for the visitors with a desperate shoestring tackle which flipped Fireball high in the air and down on the State forty-five-yard line. So, on the first play of the second half, the home fans had something to cheer about. The thunder of approval was so deafening that Lansing was forced to shout the signals in the huddle.

The cadence of Lansing's voice, as he hurried the

team out of the huddle and sent Gibbons tearing through right tackle, seemed to blend with the momentum of Fireball's mad dash. Gibbons' plunge was good for five yards and placed the ball on the mid-field stripe.

"Concentrate on Tims' strategy, now," Chip muttered to himself. "Don't miss a trick!"

Chip got a shocker right off the bat. On second down, five yards to go, Tims shot a high, spot pass to Whittemore right over the line. It was a surprise play and it clicked for four yards. Boots Cole was hurt on the play, and Speed was out on the field before Ralston could say "Morris!"

Murph Kelly helped Cole to the bench, and when time was in, it was third down and a yard to go. Chip and every fan in the stadium knew what the next play would be—Finley on a buck! But Lansing crossed up Chip, and the fans, and Brandon's forward wall as well. He sent all one hundred and seventy pounds of Speed Morris flashing straight through the left tackle slot and the Valley Falls flash went all the way to the Brandon thirty-five before the surprised secondary could bring him down.

Brandon called for time then, and Chip thought it over. He was learning fast. Lansing had used his scatback on a quick-opening play through the *weak* side tackle instead of sending one of his heavy line plungers, Fireball or Ace, through the *strong* side of the power zone.

When time was in, Lansing fooled Chip again. He used Speed again! Sent the speedster scampering through right tackle on a cross buck with a trap on Brandon's left tackle.

Speed broke into daylight and went all the way. Biggie Cohen made the "key" block on the ten-yard line, mowing the Brandon left halfback down with a crash which knocked the unfortunate visitor clear out of bounds.

Chip was on his feet, cheering and mulling over this bit of strategy, when an elbow crashed into his ribs and nearly knocked him back over the bench.

"Get goin'!" Soapy hissed, pushing him toward the field. "You deaf? Ralston's sendin' you in to kick the extra point. What's the matter with you?"

Chip grabbed his helmet and cast a frantic glance at Ralston. The big coach was looking right at him and that was enough for Chip, right or wrong! He tore across the field, thumping Lansing on the back on the way. "Great, Tims!" he shouted. "Great!" And Chip meant it with all his heart.

With Speed holding, Chip booted a perfect placement and started back up the field, his spirits revived. He'd show Ralston a little of Chip Hilton's brand of field generalship. He glanced at the scoreboard: Visitors 14, State 7. It didn't look so bad, now. State was back in the ball game!

Brandon elected to receive and Chip gave the boot all he had. But he got a little too far under the ball and it went high in the air, spinning end over end and down to the Brandon quarterback on the ten-yard line. Mike Brennan made the tackle on the fifteen, and Chip turned to drop back to the safety position. Then he saw Tims Lansing running in his direction. "Oh, no," he breathed.

"Sorry, Hilton," Lansing said, jerking his thumb toward the side-line. "Nice boot!"

Chip heard the "Hilton! Yea Hilton!" from the State cheering section but the ache was back in his chest. Soapy and Red and the rest of the bench gave him a standing ovation as he hustled past Ralston and this time he heard the coach.

"Nice going, Hilton," Ralston said. "Thanks!"

Soapy greeted Chip like a long-lost brother. "That's more like it!" he gritted. "Now you get ready! Ralston's gonna send you in the next time we get the ball! Wait and see!"

Chip kept his eyes fixed on every move Tims Lansing made. The veteran quarterback had taught him a lot in that touchdown drive. Now, he'd let Tims teach him a bit about defensive play.

Lansing was standing loosely on the Brandon thirty-five-yard line, hands on hips, nonchalantly looking at the crowd. Then, while Brandon was in the huddle, he deliberately turned his back and sauntered slowly toward the left side-line. When the visitors came up to the line, they were in their regular single-wing formation and Chip shifted his attention back to Lansing.

Suddenly, to Chip's complete surprise, Lansing turned and sprinted for the Brandon goal. Then Chip got it! And, almost as soon, the State fans roared in alarm. The Brandon tailback had dropped back and booted a low spiral, fast and far upfield; a quick-kick designed to set State far back in its own territory.

Chip focused on Lansing's speeding figure and grinned in admiration. Tims had pulled another fast one. He had fooled the Brandon quarterback by his careless attitude while the visitors were in their huddle. His carelessness had all been an act! Tims was almost as good an actor as Soapy. . . .

An explosive roar from the stands told the story. Lansing took the quick-kick over his shoulder at mid-field and, on the dead run, circled back along the side-line in front of State's bench. Miraculously, State blockers appeared all over the field, and Tims tore straight down the side-line to the Brandon twenty before he was knocked out of bounds.

Chip was cheering the wonderful run and thumping Soapy on the back when he suddenly realized the stadium had quieted. Lansing hadn't gotten up!

"No," Chip cried. "Oh, no! Not after *that* play!"

Lansing was surrounded by the officials and a knot of players from both teams now, and a dead silence

hung over the stadium. Ralston and Rockwell had nearly reached the scene when Murph Kelly stood up and beckoned. There was a short consultation, and a moment later Tims was carried toward the runway on a stretcher by two of Murph Kelly's assistants. Ralston, Doc Terring, team physician, and Murph Kelly followed. Rockwell came back, shaking his head, and nodded to Chip.

Then, as the little group accompanying Lansing turned into the tunnel leading to the locker room, the stadium came to life and cheered the great quarterback to the skies. Soapy was gripping Chip's arm and shaking him. But all of Chip's pep had fled. He didn't want to capitalize on Tims' misfortune. . . .

Brennan's keen eyes measured Chip when he trotted into the huddle. "It's all right, Chip," he said understandingly. "We know how you feel. S'pose we just win this one for Tims! Right now!"

State didn't win it right then. But they did tie it up. Brandon's line and secondary defense had tightened up in expectation of State's power offense. But Chip took a page from Lansing's book and raced out to the right behind his backs, as though for an end run. Five yards from the side-line he slid to a stop and hit Whittemore with a hard, waist-high pass behind the line of scrimmage. Chip put everything he had into that throw. He was determined that no Brandon player was going to hold that toss, even if he did get his hands on the ball.

Whittemore grunted when the ball plugged into his belly, but he held it and bulled his way to the fourteen. That made it second and four. On the next play Chip avoided the obvious, as he seemingly used the same play. This time, however, he handed off to Gibbons just before faking the same pass, and the big back circled back and tore around the left side of the line on a naked reverse. Ace was hit on the five-yard line, but he bucked and fought and forged ahead to fall across the goal line for the score.

State's cheering section went mad. Then, when Chip booted the extra point to tie the score at 14–14, the air over the whole stadium was filled with hats, coats, blankets, newspapers, shoes, and programs. And the happy fans were still at it when Chip lined up behind the ball for the kick-off.

Chip's spirits soared. It was a new ball game! He met the ball just right and it cleared the end zone, lit on the cinder track, and rolled clear to the stadium wall. It was a mighty boot and indicative of State's new strength. Before Brandon could put the ball in play, the quarter ended and the teams changed goals.

Rockwell sent Smith in for Clark, McCarthy for Anderson, and Schwartz for Higgins. The newcomers were eager and fresh and the State forward line now averaged over two hundred pounds per man. But it wasn't the weight which made the difference. It was the spirit and the hustle and fight which the newcomers displayed. Brandon put the ball in play on the twenty-yard line and couldn't do a thing. State's weight and determination began to tell and the visitors were forced to kick.

The Brandon kicker got away a high, tricky punt which carried to the State forty. Chip was surrounded and called for a fair catch. The clock showed twelve minutes to play, and Chip promptly punted back, angling the ball out of bounds on the Brandon eight-yard line. The State forwards held again and the visitors couldn't gain a foot. Brandon punted to mid-field and Chip returned the compliment. This time, the ball rolled out of bounds on the visitors' three-yard line. Two Brandon line thrusts were piled up without the gain of an inch and when the kicker dropped back to punt he was standing deep in his own end zone.

Kicking from the end zone is tough at any time. But when the game is drawing to a close and the opponents' forwards are fighting and charging and rushing every pass from center, it is plain suicide. This time, the kicker was lucky to get the ball away. It slithered off his foot, barely missing the charging State line, and went spinning out of bounds on the Brandon eighteen.

So, the exchange of punts had paid off and Chip chalked up another bit of thanks for Tims Lansing. The ball rested on Brandon's eighteen-yard line and it seemed to Chip that fifty thousand fans were chanting in unison, "We want a touchdown! We want a touchdown! We want a touchdown!"

Brandon was far from through. The visitors still had plenty of fight. State did push the ball to the Brandon six-yard line on a short pass to Whittemore and two line plunges by Fireball and Gibbons. It was first and goal to go and it looked like a cinch. But the visitors, fighting like madmen, knocked one of Chip's high end-zone passes away from Whittemore, hit Gibbons behind the line for a three-yard loss when he slipped, and held Finley to a four-yard gain off right tackle. That made it fourth down and goal to go, with less than a minute to play. It was now or never!

Chip had called his plays with an eye to a winning place-kick, and when State formed their huddle back on the fifteen-yard line for the last play, the ball was almost in the center of the field. Mike Brennan held out one hand for the team clasp and clipped Chip softly on the chin with the other. There was no need to call the play.

"We'll hold 'em, Chip!" Mike promised. "Take your time."

There really wasn't much to it. State's big line held like a stone wall and Speed took care of the rest, handling the ball perfectly and spotting it just right. Chip could have kicked that one with his eyes closed.

The thunder from the stands dwindled to the rumble of a distant passing train just before Chip booted the ball between the posts, over the track and the stadium boxes, and high up into the stands. Then the rumble exploded into a deafening roar.

No one ever knew who got the ball and no one cared! Chip was mobbed by his teammates, and Rockwell had a tough time keeping the bench off the field. There was time left for one play but Chip kicked the new ball over the end zone again and Brandon had to settle for a long, uncompleted pass from the twenty-yard line and the game was over. The final score: State 17, Brandon 14.

CHAPTER 5

TROT OUT THE HEROES

BEDLAM broke loose on the final gun. The fans started their throwing act again and those who had exhausted their ammunition spilled out on the field. One courageous group assaulted the steel disappearing goal posts at the scoreboard end of the field and others mobbed the players. Chip was marooned from his teammates by a crew of old grads.

"Hey!" one shouted. "It's Number 44! It's the quarterback!"

"That's Hilton! He won the game!"

"Hooray for Hilton! Give him a cheer, you guys!"

In a second Chip was the center of a milling crowd of cheering fans who persisted in trying to get him up on their shoulders. Chip fought them off and tried to keep moving. One old gentleman grabbed his arm in a vise-like grip and waved a program in his face. "You've got to sign this for my grandson, Hilton. He's a quarterback, too! Hey, quit shoving for a minute. Got to get this boy's autograph for my grandson. Best quarterback in the country!"

Chip eventually made the runway and the tunnel

and the door of the dressing room. There he was blocked again by a crowd of enthusiasts who were jammed right up against the door. Inside, Chip could hear his teammates celebrating. Then he was recognized and rushed again. He finally fought his way through and pounded on the door. Murph Kelly cautiously inched the door open and pulled him inside. "Look who's here!" he bellowed.

Chip's previous mauling had been mild indeed. He was greeted with a barrage of shoes, helmets, pads, socks, and jerseys, and then carried and pushed and dragged to the shower and unceremoniously shoved under the water, uniform and all. Kelly thrust a towel in his hands when he came out. That gave Chip his first chance to ask the question that had been in his mind ever since they had carried Lansing from the field.

"How is Tims? Is it bad?"

His teammates sobered and crowded around Kelly while he reported on Lansing's condition. "Has a concussion. The doctors can't tell how bad it is until they take some x-rays. He seemed all right. Coach was still with him when I left."

Few of the players who had played in that hectic last quarter realized that Ralston hadn't been on the bench. The others had been so engrossed that they hadn't given it any thought. All were amazed.

"You mean he didn't even see us win?"

"How about that? Left the game and went to the hospital with Tims!"

"Boy, that's one for the book! What a guy!"

"Who ran the team?"

"*Rockwell!* You ought to know! He put you in the game!"

"I didn't realize that. What do you know!"

Murph Kelly's report ended the celebrating in State's dressing room. Tims Lansing was popular with everyone. Chip and Soapy and Whitty and Fireball dressed hurriedly. Outside, they found the same confusion they had left on the field. Many of the happy motorists had joined the student snake dance, and the long line was now leaving the stadium and heading for town. Cars were facing in every direction, hopelessly snarled up, horns blaring and adding to the commotion.

"We'll have to walk," Fireball said wearily. "You couldn't get a taxi here to save your neck."

"Couldn't make any time anyway," Chip said cheerfully. "Come on. We'll walk."

"What's your hurry?" Whitty complained, matching Chip's long strides. "It's only five o'clock. We've got an hour."

"Chip's got business," Soapy explained. "Don't you remember the two-man, teen-age picket line? Hey, wonder if I can say that again? Two-age, teen— Aw, heck with it."

Tony and Bucky weren't in sight when they got to State Drug, and Chip forget all about them when the staff gathered around the four warriors.

"We heard it on the radio. Gee-Gee Gray got so excited when Chip made the field goal he couldn't talk!"

"What's the dope on Lansing? Hurt bad?"

Just then the student victory parade and its accompanying pandemonium arrived at Main and Tenth and began to break up. Most of the celebrants headed for State Drug.

"Here they come!" Soapy shouted. "Duck!"

Chip headed for the privacy of the stockroom with Soapy, Whitty, and Fireball at his heels. There they found seats and relaxed, weary but happy. They could hear loud-demanding voices outside.

"C'mon, Grayson! We know he's back there. Give us a break!"

"Trot 'em out, George. Trot out the heroes!"

"We won't leave till you produce Hilton. That's a promise!"

Soapy opened the door and peered out. "Lookit that mob," he said. "They've got George Grayson backed up against the soda fountain."

Finley joined Soapy at the door. "Looks as if we're in for it, Chip. Here comes Mr. Grayson."

"You mean Chip's in for it," Whitty corrected. "Me, I'm too happy right where I am. Besides, they want Chip."

"Me!" Chip remonstrated. "Why me?"

George Grayson opened the door, smiling and shaking his head apologetically. "Sorry, fellows. I can't do anything with them. Maybe you'd better come out for a second before they wreck the store." He preceded the boys and they reluctantly followed. The crowd immediately set up a good-natured howl.

" 'Ray, Hilton! Speech!"

"Yea, Soapy! Nice goin', Fireball! Atta boy, Whitty!"

Chip refused to make a speech, but Soapy wasn't so modest. The happy-go-lucky redhead climbed up behind the fountain and grinningly obliged. "You see," he began, "it was like this! Comin' out for the second half I grabs Curly Ralston by the arm. You all know Curly, of course. He's the guy who's got the best seat in the stadium and never sits down. All the guys call him Coach but he's just plain ol' Curly to me. Ahem!

"Well, anyway, I grabs my old pal by the arm and

I says: 'Curly, you wanta win this game?' He looks at me kinda funny and I says: 'Look, Curly, you ain't runnin' this team right. In the first place, you're lettin' Brandon make all the touchdowns—' "

Just then, Chip caught sight of two familiar figures on the edge of the crowd. Tony Carlara and Bucky Husta were watching the proceedings, their faces expressing utter contempt. Chip moved slowly behind the counter next to the fountain and out the side-door. Then he walked briskly up Tenth to Main and in the front door. He was standing directly behind Tony and Bucky when Soapy finished his speech and the crowd gave the popular comedian an appreciative cheer.

Tony turned away disgustedly and saw Chip standing beside him. The boy's black eyes opened wide with surprise and then narrowed. Recovering his poise quickly, he looked at Husta and said, "Well, what d'ya know! The big football hero!"

Chip grinned. "The name's Hilton," he said easily. "I've been looking for you fellows. I want to talk to you. How about joining me for a malted?"

The boys began to back away and Chip continued quickly. "Not here! At that little restaurant right down the block on Tenth. What do you say?"

Tony looked at Bucky and shrugged his shoulders. "Why not?" he said. "What have we got to lose?"

Chip led the way out the door and down Tenth to the little restaurant in the middle of the block. The silence was awkward and he tried to make conversation. "I take it you don't like football."

"Kid stuff!" Tony said shortly.

Chip was known in the restaurant and the counterman smiled and jerked his head toward the radio on the little shelf in the corner. "Talking about you, Hilton. Ears burning?"

Chip smiled and shook his head. "No. Hope it's good."

There were several customers seated at the counter and they turned to look at Chip. "You Chip Hilton?" one demanded.

Chip nodded. "That's right."

The man got up and extended his hand. "Put it there, feller. That was some game you played this afternoon. Heard it on the radio. Gee-Gee Gray says you're the greatest." He grinned and gestured toward Tony and Bucky. "These guys on the team?"

Chip smiled. "Not yet. Just friends."

Tony grunted and slouched down in one of the wooden booths which lined the wall opposite the counter. Bucky slid in beside him.

"Want the usual, Chip?" the counterman called.

"Yes, Pete, thanks. Make up a couple of malteds, too." He turned to his companions. "I'm having a hamburger. How about you?"

When Tony and Bucky declined, Chip again tried to get the conversation going. "Either of you fellows still interested in the job?"

Tony answered for both. "Us? Uh-*uh!* We're not interested."

"You have any idea why no one else has tried to get the job?"

Tony grinned knowingly. "Maybe I have and maybe I haven't," he said mysteriously.

Pete brought the sandwich and malteds then, and Chip took advantage of the interruption to think it over. It was tough going but he felt he was making progress. Tony was the dominant figure and knew all the answers. Bucky was Tony's "yes" man all right, but was not to be underestimated. He was older, bigger, and appeared tougher than Tony.

Chip decided to try an indirect attack. "I've got a tough job up there, Tony, and I need help. I'll appreciate it a lot if you can help me out. You must know *somebody* who needs a job."

Tony took his time answering, sipping his malted, and obviously thinking it over. Finally he looked Chip directly in the eye. "You're gonna have trouble gettin' someone, Mister. And if you get someone, he won't stick."

"Why?"

Tony shrugged. "Just because."

Chip's patience was nearly exhausted but he controlled the angry words which leaped to his lips and tried again. "Not even if you recommended him?"

That hit home. Tony's black eyes brightened and his tightly held lips loosened a bit, showing his sparkling white teeth. Chip waited, his pulse speeding up as he recognized the signs. Tony liked a pat on the back but Chip could tell he wouldn't have admitted the fact for the world.

"What kind of a boy do you want?" Tony demanded abruptly.

"A boy who needs help, Tony. I'd like to give the job to someone who helps out at home. Some boy who isn't afraid to work."

Tony hooked a thumb at Bucky. "Not like us, eh?"

Chip grinned. "Frankly, no!"

Tony thought about that for a few seconds. Then he pushed Bucky out of the way and stood up. "I'll think about it," he said gravely, fishing a half dollar out of his pocket and laying it on the table. "C'mon, Bucky."

Chip stood up and reached for the half dollar. "Wait a minute. I want to ask you something. How did you know I was the one to see about the job?"

Tony smiled. "That's easy. The cashier said all the applicants had to see you. She said no one else would do."

Chip held out the half dollar. "Here's your money. It's my treat. I asked *you.*"

Tony waved his hand magnanimously. "Aw, leave it for the tip," he said, swaggering toward the door.

Chip left shortly afterward and hurried through the Tenth Street entrance of State Drug. Soapy's sharp eyes spotted him as he dashed back to the stockroom. "Where you been?" he demanded excitedly. "Why don't you tell a fellow where you're goin'? Guess what! Ralston was in! He said he wanted to thank you and the rest of us for our part in pullin' the game out of the fire. How about *that?* Said he knew we could do it and wished he could have seen it.

"Another thing! Tims Lansing's O.K. Coach said the x-rays were clear and he'd be all right in a couple of days. Suggested we drop in at the hospital to see him tomorrow afternoon. He said Tims wanted 'specially to see you. Wonder what that's all about? Gosh! I gotta run! We're swamped! Never saw such a mob. See you later."

Chip was swamped, too. He was kept busy until after ten o'clock. He had just sat down to write up some orders for supplies when there was a soft knock on the door. "Come in," he called.

There were two of them. The oldest boy was about fifteen and slight of build. Chip judged that he weighed ninety pounds or so. He had blue eyes, brown hair, and an upturned nose. The other boy was a smaller edition, with the exception that he was better put together. He had the same blue eyes and light hair but his nose was definitely pug. Chip figured that he was nine or maybe ten years old. Both were dressed plainly but their clothes were clean.

The older boy hesitated and then spoke in a low, half-fearful voice. "The lady at the desk said to see you." The boy was shy and seemed able to speak only because of some special urgency.

Chip smiled. "About the job?"

"Yes, sir. I—"

"Is this your brother?"

"Yes, sir."

"It's pretty late for you two fellows to be out, isn't it? Your mother know where you are?"

"Our mother's dead, sir. But Aunt Edith knows where we are. She lives with us."

"Where's your father?"

The boy squirmed. "He's home, I guess, sir."

"You mean you're allowed out this late?" Chip persisted.

"Yes, sir. No, sir. That is, I have to have a job, sir, and I—that is Mark and I—thought if I came tonight I might have a better chance." He thrust his hand into the pocket of his coat. "Here's my permit to work, sir. I—I'm a good worker. I've had a paper route for five years. Mark has it now."

"Mark?"

"Yes, sir. My brother, here. He's Mark." The boy hesitated and then continued with more confidence. "Mark has been helping me with the route a long time. He knows the route better than I do. We decided I could help him with most of the deliveries and then get down here and take over this job."

"What's *your* name?"

"Eddie, sir. Eddie Redding."

"How did you find out about the job, Eddie?"

The boy hesitated. "Why—why all the boys in our neighborhood knew about it, sir. We're not very far away, sir. Just a few blocks."

"You can call me Chip, Eddie. I like it better."

"Yes, sir, Chip."

"Do you have to help out at home, Eddie?"

"Oh, yes, sir. Pop has a hard time finding work and I have to bring money home to help Aunt Edith. Sometimes we don't have any money for groceries at all."

That struck home. "All right, Eddie," Chip said brusquely. "I'll give you the job on a trial basis." He handed the boy an application blank. "Sit down there at the desk and fill it out." He turned to Mark. "Would you like some ice cream or a soda or something?"

Mark glanced at his brother. "I sure would," he said, his face lighting up with a slow grin.

Chip grinned back and headed for the fountain. The crowd had thinned out and the clerks were getting ready to close up. Chip glanced at the clock. Ten minutes to eleven. It was too late for a boy to be out even if he did have late-hour working papers. Why, at home, in Valley Falls, the kids had to be off the streets by nine o'clock. He could remember the kids streaking for home as soon as they heard the nine-o'clock siren. Parents really laid it on a fellow in those days when the curfew caught him out late. . . .

Chip was at the fountain now, and Soapy grinned when his pal asked him for two big vanilla cones and two black-and-white sodas and told Soapy to put it on his account. "Anything you say, pal. You hire 'em both?"

"Wish I could," Chip said. "I really wish I could."

Ten minutes later Chip's new assistant and his big-little brother had finished their refreshments. Chip read through the application blank and then handed Eddie the job description he had prepared. "This outlines your duties, Eddie. Study it hard. Now, come on out and meet the rest of the staff."

Chip introduced Eddie and Mark to Mitzi Savrill, the cashier, George Grayson, and the fountain crew. "Pretty late for you fellows to be out, isn't it?" Soapy asked.

Chip answered for the boys. "It sure is! Come on, Eddie. We'll walk you home."

Eddie's face flooded scarlet and a half-scared expression flashed across his face. "No, sir, please. We'd like to go home by ourselves, sir. If you don't mind, sir. We have to—"

"Have to?"

"Yes, sir. It's only four blocks. I'll report Monday, sir." Eddie backed hastily away, pulling Mark by the arm. "I'll report right after we finish with the papers, sir—er, Chip. Just like you said. Good night—"

CHAPTER 6

A PROJECT FOR SOAPY

SOAPY SMITH had grown up in the same neighborhood, attended the same grade school, and played on the same high school team with Chip Hilton, his best pal and personal hero. Soapy was a charter member of the Hilton A.C., and was as much at ease in the Hilton home as in his own. Furthermore, the two friends were roommates at Jeff and shared their fortunes, good or bad. The long friendship had enabled them to acquire a sort of mental telepathy where mutual understanding was concerned, and it went into high gear right after the two Redding boys departed.

When Chip told Fireball and Whitty that he was going on ahead on some personal business and would join them later at Pete's restaurant, Soapy knew instantly what Chip had in mind. The redhead sauntered out of the store and turned the corner. Chip caught up with him at the end of the first block.

"They're on the other side of the street," Soapy said. "Boy, this is *some* neighborhood!"

"It's that, all right," Chip agreed. "It seems as if the tenement districts are always close to the principal section of a city."

"You're right," Soapy agreed. "Guess the center of a town just moves away from the oldest buildings and the poor people move in. You ever see a darker street? I'd be afraid to walk down here alone myself. Hey, the kids have stopped. Look at that! Look at all the kids on that corner. Must be twenty of them. Where's the cops? Why don't they make those kids go home?"

"It's a mystery to me," Chip said. "Hold it. Let's stop here a minute."

Soapy grasped Chip by the arm. "Look, Chip. Eddie is talking to that Tony— What's his name?"

"Carlara," Chip added.

"What's the name of the other one?"

"Bucky. Bucky Husta."

"Those kids ought to be home in bed," Soapy grumbled. "It's nearly twelve o'clock. Good thing for us there's no training curfew on Saturday nights! What in the world are their parents thinking of to leave kids out this late at night?"

Chip was watching the group, hardly listening to Soapy. Eddie was talking to Tony Carlara and Chip figured he was explaining that he'd gotten the job. But why . . . "Come on," he said abruptly. "Let's eat."

"O.K. How come Eddie is talking to that Tony guy, Chip?"

"I don't know, Soapy," Chip said slowly. "I don't get it."

"You think there's some connection between Eddie and those two little punks, Chip?"

"It sure looks like it. Only thing I can figure is that

Tony and Bucky made sure Eddie Redding got the job."

"How could they do that?"

"Easy. As long as someone as tough or tougher didn't come along and want the job."

"Sure, I get it! They kept the other kids away. That's why they kept waiting outside the store all the time."

"I think so. But why? Why Eddie Redding?"

"Got me. But you know something, Chip. I think Eddie is O.K."

Chip nodded in the darkness. "Yes, Soapy, he does seem all right. But somehow I can't figure Eddie being the type who would be friendly with boys like Tony Carlara and Bucky Husta."

"Is that bad? Heck, he seems to me like the kind of a kid you wanted to get the job."

"He is, Soapy. That is, if he told me the truth. But there's something else. You remember Louie Edwards and Red Fleming? You remember how they bullied every kid in the neighborhood until they made the mistake of picking on Biggie's brother?"

"Sure I remember! And I remember the time they tried to pick on you, too. What's this got to do with Louie Edwards and Red Fleming?"

"Nothing. Nothing except that Tony Carlara and Bucky Husta seem to be the same kind of kids. Maybe I'm imagining things. Come on. Forget it."

Finley and Whittemore were waiting in the restaurant. Fireball looked up from his scrambled eggs. "That was fast," he said. "Why all the mystery?"

"Checking up on Ralston's detectives," Soapy whispered, looking around mysteriously. "They probably don't know we're allowed to break training Saturday nights."

Chip didn't join in the conversation. He was trying to figure out why Eddie Redding had been so secretive about his relationship with Tony Carlara and Bucky Husta. He was still thinking about it when he got back to Jeff and went to bed.

Soapy was right on the ball at seven o'clock Sunday morning, but he disturbed only his Valley Falls pals. He surprised them, too, when he soberly advised them they could "sleep-in" after they read the paper. Then he presented each with a paper opened to the sports page where a three-column picture showed Chip Hilton kicking the winning field goal in the Brandon game.

Chip didn't like all the publicity and particularly Soapy's part in advertising it. He took a long walk alone and then went to church. Afterward, he joined his friends at the Tenth Street restaurant for lunch and then the whole crowd walked up to the hospital to see Tims Lansing. Tims was sitting up in bed reading a paper when they were admitted to his room. He greeted them warmly.

"Nice going, gang," Tims said. "Some comeback!" He winked toward Chip and poked a finger at the paper. "You're better looking," he said, grinning.

Other teammates dropped in from time to time, and when the nurse poked her head in the door and advised the players who crowded the room that time was up, Lansing asked Chip to wait a couple of minutes. "You fellows mind if I speak to Chip alone?" he asked.

When the others had gone, Lansing motioned Chip to a chair. "I guess you're wondering what this all is about. . . .

"Well, it's about you. You're a great football player, Chip. The best I ever saw. You can do everything. I guess you're going to think this is funny, coming from me, but I think you can be even better. What I'm trying to say is awkward because—well, I don't know you very well—"

Chip smiled and interrupted. "If it's about football and running a team on the field and pulling a game out of the fire," he said, grinning, "believe me, I'll listen all night. You taught me a lot yesterday, Tims, whether you know it or not." Chip checked Lansing when the veteran quarterback remonstrated. "Yes, you did, Tims.

"I watched you every second yesterday in that second half before you got hurt. Why, I can call every play you used right now, every one of them. I made so many mistakes in that first half it was pitiful. I ran the legs off the team back where it didn't count. Then when we got up where we needed the push, we were out of gas."

Lansing shook his head. "I wasn't going to criticize, Chip. I didn't mean that. You see, I know just what Ralston expects from his quarterback because I learned it the hard way. I thought maybe I could help you by going over some game situations and checking the proper plays. Why, if we could get together an hour a day you'd have it down pat by Saturday. Would you like to do it?"

"And how! You just set the time."

It was agreed that Chip should come to the hospital during his free periods until Tims got out. Then they would make other arrangements. Chip's pals were waiting for him at the hospital entrance and they walked slowly back to Jeff. Chip spent the rest of the afternoon and evening "hitting the books."

Curly Ralston and his coaching staff got as much of a lift from the last-ditch victory over Brandon as the team. A new spirit seemed to grip every player on the squad. It was obvious in their bearing and in their new confidence in handling the ball and running the plays.

Chip spent every possible minute with Tims, and a strong friendship developed between the two. Then Tims got his discharge with the understanding that he would not practice nor play for a week. On Thursday, after practice and following a discussion of the Carlton scouting notes, Ralston excused the squad with the exception of Chip, Buzz Burk, and Mike McGuire. Burk and McGuire had been used at quarterback all week and Chip knew that Ralston was taking no chance on another injury leaving him without a replacement. Chip mentally thanked Tims Lansing when Ralston began to shoot questions fast and furious at the three quarterbacks.

"When do you use trap plays, Hilton?"

"Only when opponents expect a big yardage play, Coach."

"Explain that!"

"Well, when opponents expect you to try for small yardage, say up to four yards for a first down, they concentrate on line defense and use a seven- or eight-man line in one alignment or another to beat the trap."

Ralston shot a quick glance at Burk and McGuire. "Got that?" he demanded. "Understand it?"

Burk and McGuire nodded and Ralston grunted approvingly. "All right, Hilton. Now, speaking of small yardage, when should you use a slow-developing play?"

"Never on the first down, Coach. And seldom on a small yardage situation unless it goes to the outside."

"Why?"

"Hard-charging opponents can break through and throw the ball carrier for a loss if there is much delay on a play."

"Now, Burk, suppose the opponents are using what we call a magnetic line. What kind of plays would be best?"

Burk had spent a lot of time studying the plays, but it was evident that he was not used to the quick thinking which is a must with a quarterback. "Er—magnetic means a waiting line, Coach, and I guess the best plays would be through the line or around the ends. If they're waiting, it means they will have time to drop back for passes or meet the point of attack if we don't smash."

Ralston hesitated. "Well, that's partly right. What do you say, McGuire?"

"I think all the plays should be straight, hard-smashing line slants, Coach."

Ralston nodded vigorously. "Right! Run 'em off the field when they start waiting! Now, McGuire, what if the field is wet and the ball is slippery? What kind of plays would you use?"

McGuire hesitated. "I've heard you say a lot of times, Coach, that we shouldn't try to pass too much and that we ought to use simple plays and avoid double ball-handling as well as wide runs."

"That's right! Now, Hilton, on small yardage, assuming you want a first down, where is the best point of attack under our style of play?"

Chip could almost see Tims Lansing using that play against Brandon. Tims and he had discussed that very situation in the back of the library right after lunch. "To the short side, Coach. Inside the defensive left end or tackle."

Ralston grinned. "Had your eyes open in that third

quarter on Saturday, didn't you? Good! Now, Hilton, while you're answering the questions, if you're in a tight spot and need a couple of yards for a mighty important first down, what would govern your choice of the play?"

"Two or three things, sir. Our position on the field, the down, the alignment of the defense—"

Ralston waved a hand in protest. "I'm talking about the player to carry the ball as much as I am the play, Hilton."

"Yes, sir. I'd use the back who had been doing the best running, and I'd call the play he had been running most successfully."

That answer pleased Ralston but it didn't stop the questions. He snapped them out and kept it up for the better part of an hour. "Good," he said finally. "Now, one last question. When is the best time to pass? You answer that, Hilton."

"I think the best time to pass is on small-yardage downs, Coach. Such as second down and three yards to go for a first down. Taking the time to play, the score, and the position on the field into consideration, naturally."

Ralston seemed satisfied. "Wait a second, boys. This *is* the last. Now, Hilton, how do you camouflage your best deep pass?"

"It should be on a small-yardage down, sir. And it should look like an end run to the wide side of the field and with the fullback or one of the halfbacks throwing the ball. Finley is a good passer, sir, and I think I would use him to throw the ball if I were calling the plays."

Ralston rose to his feet. "Thanks, men. We'll continue this some other time. That's all."

Chip was fifteen minutes late when he arrived at

the drugstore, but Eddie had everything under control. Eddie hustled every minute. In fact, he was so devoted to his work that Chip didn't have the heart to ask about Carlara and Husta. So Chip decided to concentrate on the big-little Redding. Mark always dropped around to help Eddie, but Chip figured he was chiefly interested in the banana splits and other concoctions Soapy and Fireball and Whitty bought for him. Chip did manage to get Mark to invite him to visit the Redding home next Sunday afternoon.

Eddie surprised Chip later that evening. He busied himself unnecessarily in the stockroom for a few minutes and then blurted out, "I wish I was a football player."

"You can be," Chip assured him. "If you put on some weight and learn to handle yourself on a football field. Come here. Let's see how much you *do* weigh? Hmmm. Ninety-five pounds. That's not very much, is it? Let's see. We might as well start with posture. Turn around.

"Push your shoulders straight back. Good. Now, when I count, breathe in—one, two, three. Out—one, two, three. In—one, two, three. Get it? Now you practice that until I get back. Remember, shoulders straight *back*, not *up!*"

Out at the fountain, Soapy listened enthusiastically as Chip told him about Eddie. "You mean he can be my special project?" Soapy demanded. "Well, you just watch! Wait till I put him on the ol' Soapy Smith plan. I'll have him as fat as Tiny Tim McCarthy before Christmas. Wait and see? I'll start right now! Be back in a minute."

Chip went back to the stockroom and Soapy appeared almost on his heels with a big container. "Drink this!" Soapy said, ruffling Eddie's hair. "You're gonna eat three of these every night, compliments of your coaching staff, Fireball Finley, Whitty Whittemore, and yours truly. O.K.?"

Chip and his State Drug crew didn't fool around after closing that night. The team was leaving for Carlton at noon the next day and it was important that every player be home before the eleven-o'clock curfew.

There was a big crowd of fans at the railroad station to see them off on Friday, and they got some fine cheers and some good advice. "Make it Number Three!" "State of the Nation, gang! Stay that way!"

After the train pulled out of University for the seven-hour ride to Carlton, Chip settled down in his seat beside Soapy and prepared for a long snooze. He had just reached the pleasant, relaxed semistupor which precedes real sleep when Soapy dug an elbow viciously in his ribs. "Now what?" Chip growled, glaring at Soapy. "What's the matter with you?"

Soapy shifted his eyes upward and then Chip saw Ralston standing in the aisle with Buzz Burk and Mike McGuire. He shot to his feet, wide awake. "Oh, Coach," he managed. "I was half asleep."

"That's all right, Hilton," Ralston said, smiling. "I thought it might be a good time for us to get together and talk a little strategy."

Soapy slide out in the aisle. "I guess you won't be needing me," he said, clearing his throat. "Now if it was a little talk about metaphysics, phrenology, craniology, or a study in castrametation. . . ."

CHAPTER 7
THE CINDERELLA KIDS

RALSTON started right in as if there had been no interruption in the skull quiz of the preceding afternoon. He began with Chip and continued the passing discussion. "We talked about the best time to pass, yesterday, Hilton, and the best way to conceal a long pass. Suppose we just continue in that vein. In what area on the field would you use a long, deep pass?"

"Anywhere between our own thirty-yard line and the opponents' thirty, Coach."

"Right. Burk, what should you do when your receivers are all covered and you are being rushed?"

Burk wasn't too sure of his answer but he tried. "Lots of passers throw the ball away in that situation, Coach. Try to ground it. But I know you don't want us to do that, so I guess I'd try to run the ball."

Ralston turned to McGuire. "What would you do, McGuire?"

"I think I'd just take the loss, Coach, rather than make a wild throw or try to run wide and be thrown for a big loss."

"Good," Ralston agreed. "That's absolutely right. Intentionally grounding a pass is against the rules and against the spirit of the game. Besides, it's dangerous. You should drive straight ahead and try to keep from losing too much ground."

"What territory is usually open in any pass defense, Hilton?"

"The zone in front of the safety man."

"That's right. It's the safest, too."

Ralston continued the quiz for another half-hour and then moved on to another group. Chip took his nap and dozed until Soapy roused him for dinner. Eating in a dining car is fun for any passenger, and Chip and Soapy enjoyed the novelty of the experience almost as much as the big, thick steak.

The train arrived in Carlton at seven o'clock, and the team took taxis to the Carlton Country Club. Then, instead of the workout they expected, Ralston led the squad on a long hike around the course. They covered the eighteen holes and came back tired and dreading another skull session. But Ralston surprised them. "We'll take the evening off, men," he said. "I'll expect you to check in at eleven-thirty sharp. They tell me that there are two or three good movies in town and that might be a good way to forget the game."

Chip and his crowd took in a movie and got back to the country club at eleven o'clock. Chip slept fitfully and awakened the next morning, lazily glad that Murph Kelly's game-day training schedule called for the first and only pre-game meal at eleven o'clock. He remained in bed until ten o'clock and then ate lightly. And, once more, he was the first man dressed for the game. This time, Chip didn't fuss with his uniform. He sat calm and collected, and planned his campaign for the afternoon. He was almost certain to start and had made up his mind to run the team according to Tim Lansing's book.

Chip got the chance. Ralston started Whittemore and Higgins at the ends, Cohen and Maxim in the tackle slots, McCarthy and Smith at the guard positions, and Captain Mike Brennan at center. The starting backfield was Morris, Gibbons, Finley, and Chip. Brennan won the toss and elected to receive. Chip moved up to the five-yard line and waited for the boot. He glanced along the line of Carlton starters. They were well set up and looked sharp. Then the kicker's toe plunked into the ball and the game was on.

The kick was short and straight into Finley's arms. Fireball dug right up the middle to the State forty-five-yard line before he was buried under a mass of blue-clad tacklers. Chip remembered Tims Lansing, and startled every player in the huddle when he called for a pass. It clicked. Whittemore was closely played by two Carlton defenders but Chip pegged the ball to him anyway. All three went up for the ball, but two long red-clad arms plucked the ball out of the air. Whitty held it as he tumbled down on the thirty.

Chip came right back with another aerial. This time he sent Fireball around right end, apparently on an end run. But Fireball chucked the ball to Higgins in the end zone and State had scored in the first two minutes of play. The Carlton stands were silent, stunned by the suddenness of the score.

Carlton came back fighting. Chip kicked to the goal line and Finley dropped the ball-carrier on the twenty-yard line. Then the home stalwarts fought their way down the field in short, desperate line plunges which were determined and irresistible. But their drive petered out before they could get into scoring territory, and State took the ball on its own thirty-five. Chip immediately punted, booting the ball in a high, spinning spiral which carried to the Carlton twenty-eight-yard line. The Carlton quarterback was surrounded by State tacklers and signaled for a fair catch. Then Carlton began pounding the line all over again, using the antiquated formula of "hit the line on first down, run the ends next, pass on third down, and kick on the fourth."

Back in the safety position, Chip shook his head. But for Tims Lansing, the tactics employed by the Carlton quarterback might well have been his own. It was bad football and it showed up in the score. State had an easy time and led, 21 to 0, at the half.

In the second half, Ralston eased up and cleared his bench. But the State replacements clicked for another touchdown and Ralston sent Chip in long enough to kick the extra point. Carlton managed to score in the last quarter and Chip booted a thirty-yard placement seconds before the end of the game. The final score: State 31, Carlton 6.

Somehow, Chip didn't feel very good about the game. The contingent of State rooters in the visitors' section celebrated the victory as a great feat, but Chip and his teammates knew the score could just as easily have been 60 to 6. Ralston just didn't believe in humiliating an opponent.

The State squad left Carlton on the midnight sleeper, but it was almost two o'clock before the happy players could relax and get to bed. Chip tumbled in early and slept like a rock.

There wasn't a sound in State's special Pullman as the train streaked through the early dawn. Therefore, it is understandable that the porter would be astonished by the appearance of a redheaded newsboy who had somehow climbed aboard the train at Dodgetown and forgotten to get off.

"Boy, you're in trouble! This here train don't stop— Oh, oh! It's you! What you doin' up this early?"

"The coach always gives me the responsibility of calling the players in the morning," Soapy assured him. "I'm the rabble-rouser!"

The porter regarded Soapy dubiously. "Where you get those papers?"

"Dodgetown. I had the conductor wire ahead. Look, you want to see a picture of the greatest football player in the world? O.K., look at this!"

"I know that feller! He's in Room 16. The one with the yellow hair. Right?"

"Yep," Soapy said proudly. "That's my roommate! Chip Hilton! Now I gotta wake up the guys and give them their papers. See you later."

Chip heard the pounding on the doors but it was not until his roommate shoved him roughly and pushed a copy of the *Herald* under his nose that he was completely awake.

"Look!" Soapy said excitedly. "Another picture! And read what Bill Bell has to say in his column. Great!"

Chip sat up slowly and regarded the picture. It had been taken in the first game of the season and showed him executing his part of the Statue of Liberty play which had resulted in the winning touchdown against Tech by Philip Whittemore. "Not again," he muttered. "This is no good."

"Oh, yes it is," Soapy corrected. "Read Bill Bell's column."

"You don't understand," Chip remonstrated. "This isn't fair to the rest of the fellows. What's Bill Bell trying to do?"

"I guess he knows what he's doing," Soapy said complacently. "He's been writing sports for forty years."

"I don't mean that."

"Aw, c'mon, Chip. Remember what I told you when we were sitting on the bench in the Brandon game. You play like Chip Hilton ought to play all the time and let the blocks fall whom they may. You hear?"

Chip read the caption under the picture. *William "Chip" Hilton, State quarterback, setting up play which won thriller first game from Tech.* Then Chip shifted over to Bill Bell's column.

STATE ROLLS OVER CARLTON, 31–6

By Bill Bell

Carlton, *October 16.*—State's powerful, quick-striking team made it three in a row here this afternoon. Much of the credit for the easy victory goes to Curly Ralston's sophomore quarterback sensation who called his plays perfectly. Hilton's opening-play pass struck with devastating speed and the second aerial, pegged by Finley to Higgins, was good for a touchdown before half of the fans in the Carlton Stadium realized the game was under way. Hilton then kicked the extra point and State led, 7–0, before the game was two minutes old.

Overmatched Carlton made a gallant fight of it when they had the ball, but State had too many guns for the home town forces. State won its third game of the season, 31 to 6, before 33,184 spectators.

Last year, you may remember, this writer tabbed an

unknown pilot in the University Dorm League as the greatest varsity prospect he had ever seen. The player, Chip Hilton, pictured elsewhere on this page, quarterbacked Jeff into the dorm championship and later represented State in the frosh game against the A. & M. yearlings on Thanksgiving Day. Yes . . . it's the same youngster . . . the leader of Jeff's Cinderella Kids.

I'd like to quote from that story: "This year's championship team, Jefferson, proves something else—proves kids can work and study and still play an outstanding game. Seven of the eleven starters are working their way through college. And every player on the starting team passed his mid-term examinations with an average of 80 per cent or better . . ."

Now back to the present. . . . *Four* of the players who started for Curly Ralston at Carlton yesterday were members of that Cinderella team—and six of the Cinderella Kids are on the squad.

"What's wrong with that?" Soapy demanded, grinning happily.

Chip smiled. "I'll bet you passed these all over the train," he said reproachfully, beginning to dress. "I feel like two cents."

Soapy was demoralized. "But why, Chip? Why?"

"It isn't false modesty, Soapy. I like to see my name on the sports page just like anyone else and I'm proud to be on a State team. It's just that so much fuss makes me feel funny. It's embarrassing, that's all."

Chip soon found out that he need not worry about his teammates. They were as proud of the sports page write-up of him and his friends as they had been of his success on the field. They added their congratulations to Soapy's. "Boy, I'd give my right arm if Bill Bell would write a column like that about me!" "Let's hope he keeps writing 'em all season!"

"He will! We've got it made! A. & M., here we come!"

Chip went to church and had lunch with the Jeff crowd. Then he started out to visit the home of Eddie Redding. He strolled down Main Street and turned the corner and walked past Pete's restaurant. It was closed, so he continued on down Tenth Street four blocks until he came in sight of the candy store on the corner. A block away he recognized Tony Carlara and Bucky Husta lounging on the corner talking to several other youngsters. As Chip approached, he sensed the antagonism in the battery of eyes that surveyed him.

A stranger could have guessed which youth was the leader. Chip didn't have to be told. "Hello, Tony," he said. "Can you tell me where Eddie Redding lives?"

Tony took plenty of time answering, measuring Chip up and down as he had that first time, apparently more for effect than for any other reason. "Sure," he drawled insolently, staring boldly at Chip. "Why?"

Chip smiled, trying to conceal his irritation. "Because Eddie invited me to his house for a visit," he said patiently.

There was a long, heavy silence and Chip could feel the wall of dislike, almost hate, which seemed to spring up between the boys and himself. What was wrong with these kids? he asked himself.

Tony studied Chip a long minute and then hooked a thumb contemptuously over his shoulder. "Fourth house on the left," he said shortly, turning back to his companions.

Chip hesitated and then walked slowly away, half angry and half hurt by the treatment. He normally had little trouble making friends, and the reception he had just experienced added to his resolve to solve the mystery of Eddie Redding's association with Tony Carlara and Bucky Husta.

The Redding home was in a narrow, two-story brick house. The surrounding houses were unpainted, with worn wooden stoops which led to each doorway. The dingy basement apartments with the dirty windows and the littered steps leading to the below-level doors were hardly fit for pigs, much less human beings. Chip hesitated and then walked up the four steps which led to the ground-floor apartment. He lifted his hand to knock, but before his fist could tap the door, it flew open.

Mark greeted Chip with his slow smile. "Hi, Chips! Come on in! We been expectin' you."

Chip followed Mark back through the narrow passageway, noting the once-green runner with the ragged edges which led to a door at the end of the hall. Inside, it seemed to Chip that the whole family must be gathered in the room. A middle-aged woman was hastily clearing dishes off a table. Eddie Redding leaped from a chair where he had been reading a newspaper. Chip saw that it was the *Herald* and that it was opened to the sports page which contained his picture.

"Gee, Chip, congratulations! This is some write-up! Oh, I want you to meet my folks. This is Aunt Edith."

Chip shook hands with the tired-looking lady who smiled gently. "I'm glad to meet you, Mr. Hilton," she said softly. "I feel like I know you"—she gestured toward Eddie and Mark—"the boys talk about you so much. Won't you sit down?"

Chip sat down and then met Della, Gertrude,

Ethel, and Trinka, all younger than Mark. "That's the family," Eddie said proudly. "All except Pop. He's asleep. I'll call him."

Chip stopped him. "No, don't do that, Eddie. I'll meet him some other time." It seemed to Chip that Eddie's face registered relief.

It was a pleasant visit. Chip enjoyed the girls, and Eddie's aunt proved to be a good conversationalist. Although the surroundings were eloquent evidence of the family's financial straits, Chip heard nothing during his hour stay to indicate their difficulties. Chip was sincere when he said good-by and promised to come soon again. Eddie and Mark accompanied him from the dining-room. Just as they reached the end of the hall, a door on the left opened and a man thrust his head out.

"Where you going, Eddie, Mark?" the man demanded sharply. Then, seeing Chip, he paused uncertainly.

"This is Mr. Hilton, Pop," Eddie explained. "The man I work for—"

Redding extended his calloused hand. "Glad to meet you, Hilton," he said abruptly. He hesitated a second and then stepped back in the room. "Now don't you kids go near that trash on the corner," he said sharply. "You hear, Eddie? You hear, Mark?"

CHAPTER 8

AN OVERDOSE OF CUNNING

TONY CARLARA and his corner pals were still lounging in front of the candy store when Chip passed. But their averted glances and sudden concentration on something in the other direction made it clear that they did not care to speak. Chip continued on, thinking about Eddie. He was completely sold on his assistant and the whole Redding family. The knowledge he had gained that afternoon concerning Eddie's responsibilities was enough for Chip. His brisk pace soon brought him to Jeff, where he spent the rest of the day studying.

Football was the chief topic of conversation on the campus Monday morning, and Chip was the center of interest in his classes. He sighed with relief when his third class ended and he could start for his luncheon appointment. Tims Lansing, who was waiting outside the Student Union restaurant, welcomed him with a big smile.

"Congratulations, Chip. Nice going! I read the story of the game in the Sunday papers. It was terrific! I liked that first pass."

"Thanks to you," Chip said. "I'd never have called that pass if it wasn't for you."

Lansing grinned. "I couldn't help you now, Chip. You're a post-graduate."

"Nothing doing!" Chip protested. "I need your help now more than ever. If you can take time off from your own football."

"I'm afraid that there isn't going to be any more football for me, Chip. Doc Terring side-lined me for another three weeks. Season will be over before I can get back in shape. My football days are over."

"No!"

Lansing nodded grimly. "That's what the man said. Come on, let's eat. I'm starved."

They joined the cafeteria line and carried their trays to an unoccupied table in a corner. After they finished eating, Lansing pulled the morning paper out of his pocket and handed it to Chip. "Read what Jim Locke has to say about our chances for the conference title."

A. & M. LOOMS AS CONTENDER FOR NATIONAL HONORS

Conference Champions Win Number 12

By Jim Locke

Powerful, all-victorious A. & M. took another step this Saturday toward the national championship by racking up victory Number 12 at the expense of Brandon by a score of 33 to 6. The Farmers have won five straight this year, running wild over Wesleyan, Carlton, Tech, and Brandon, and outscoring Southwestern 30 to 13. A. & M. has scored 170 points to their opponents' 21 this season and the all-veteran team seems stronger than ever.

Local fans, unreasonably enthusiastic because of State's three-game winning streak, are beginning to compare the locals with A. & M. A comparison of scores quickly shatters the illusion. State defeated Tech by a last-second touchdown; A. & M. defeated the Engineers 28 to 2; State barely squeaked by Brandon 17 to 14; A. & M. swamped the same team 33 to 6; State beat Carlton 31 to 6; A. & M. buried the Carlton forces 51 to 0. Nuf sed?

Lansing chuckled when Chip finished reading the article. "Likes us, doesn't he?"

"Guess he likes A. & M. more," Chip said. "Can't blame him for that."

"Time will tell," Lansing said grimly. "How about a little football?"

"Right! I put in six hours of study yesterday and I'm through until time to go to practice. Let's go."

Chip spent two hours with Lansing at their favorite library table and then headed for practice. Because his muscles were stiff from the Carlton game, he was anxious to get out on the field and loosen up. On hurrying into the dressing room, he was surprised to find it deserted except for the trainer. Chip stopped and looked around. "Where's everybody, Murph? No practice today?"

"Oh, there's practice, all right. Up in the skull room. Coach is getting soft. Says you fellows need a rest. This modern game beats me. When I was a young man we played our football on the field. Now it seems about all the coaches want to do is run movies and draw pictures on a blackboard. It's sickening!"

Ralston's skull-room procedure was old stuff to State's varsity. The famous coach believed that more football games were won with brains than brawn. Soapy and Biggie were holding a chair for Chip and he sat between them. At 3:45 sharp Rockwell rapped on his chair and Ralston moved to the blackboard.

"Men," he began, "we're going to cut this practice short. But before we let you go, we want to tell you about our plans for Saturday. Southwestern is our next opponent and they're good.

"I'm sure that you know their record as well as I do, but it's wise to keep in mind that they won the Sugar Bowl game and have an all-veteran team. They've lost only to A. & M. Jim scouted them Saturday and thinks they will use a five-man defensive line because—" Ralston paused and chuckled—"because we have discovered the value of the forward pass as a part of our offense.

"Now I'm *not* going to put all our pass plays on the board to check the blocking against a five-man line, but I am going to discuss a couple of plays so we'll know what to expect." Ralston quickly chalked the play on the board.

Even a football novice would have appreciated

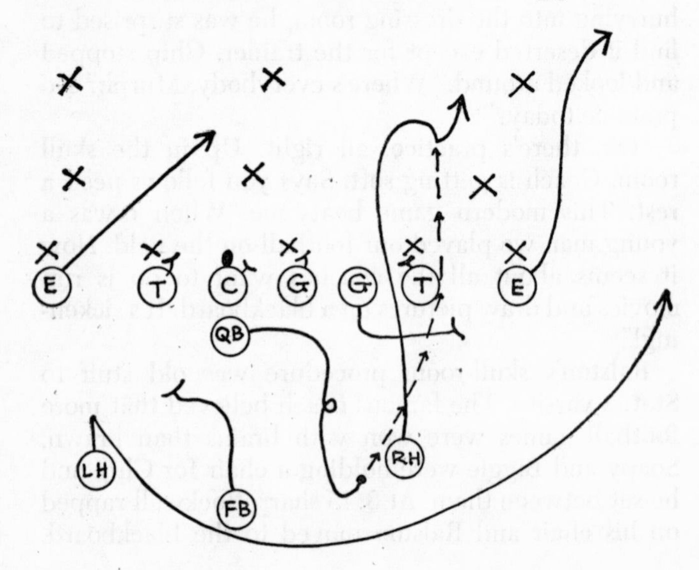

Ralston's skill at a blackboard. After completing the play, he tapped the board with the piece of chalk and continued:

"The quarterback first fakes a hand-off to the right halfback, who drives straight ahead. The second fake is to the left halfback cutting behind the quarterback and around right end. Good faking by the backs on this play is vital. The right halfback turns on the count of ten for the pass. Any questions?"

Ace Gibbons cleared his throat and raised his hand. "Coach," he said hesitantly, "the defensive left halfback hit me Saturday almost as soon as I caught the ball. Carlton was using a six-man defensive line, of course, but I was wondering if our right end couldn't cut to the outside of the backer-up on that side and get downfield a little faster. Seems as if I'm in the secondary before he is—"

Ralston nodded. "I noticed that too, Ace. It's a matter of timing. You'll have to spot-run a little longer and our right end will have to get away faster. Are there any other questions on this play? No? Good. Now the buttonhook to the left halfback."

Ralston continued talking as he chalked the second play on the board. "I guess you've gathered by this time that we intend to do a lot of passing. Exactly what Southwestern expects. And, we think the buttonhook series is the most effective type of pass we can use against a 5–3–3 defense. So we want you to think about these until tomorrow afternoon. Now, let's take a good look at the buttonhook to the left halfback.

"Now this buttonhook to the left halfback is a take-off on our fullback smash to the weak side. The faking by the backs is even more important than it is on the buttonhook to the right back. The right halfback is in motion to the left on the count of two. The quarterback first fakes to him, then to the fullback, and then cuts back to the passing slot, concealing the ball.

"The halfback and the fullback must pull good fakes and hold them for a count of eight. The ends must sprint directly toward the defensive backs and then buttonhook left or right, according to the signal. Any questions?" There was a short silence. Ralston continued, "All right then, let's keep thinking about Southwestern's 5–3–3 defense. That's all."

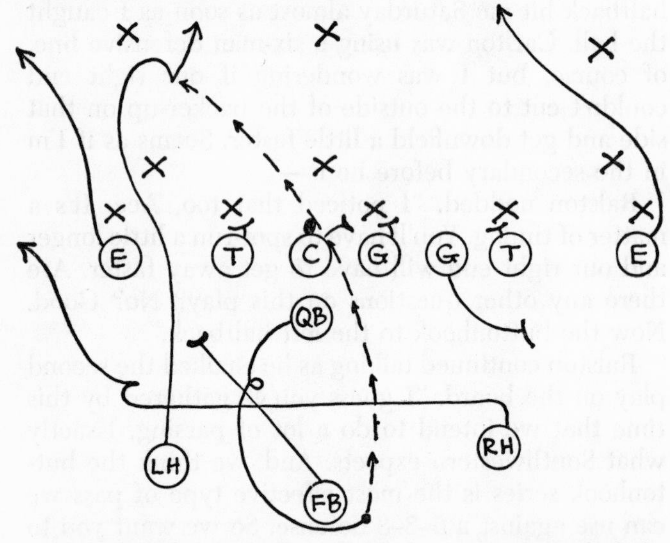

Soapy followed Chip out through the player's gate, trying to keep in step with Chip's long strides. "What's the rush?" he complained.

"Incoming deliveries! A million of them! It's the same every Monday."

Chip was surprised to find the stockroom door locked. He checked with Mitzi and learned that

Eddie had not reported. The stockroom telephone rang at six-thirty and it turned out to be his assistant. Eddie's voice was tense and anxious.

"Chip, sir, this is Eddie. I'm awful sorry, but I'm sick. I guess I can't come to work."

"What's wrong, Eddie?"

"I'm just sick. Mark said he would tell you after he finished delivering the papers but I didn't want you to worry."

"Where are you calling from, Eddie?"

"Why, the candy store."

"Did you have the doctor?"

"No, sir. I'll be all right in a couple of days, I think."

"All right, Eddie. You hurry home and stop worrying. You better get right to bed. Good night."

As Chip cradled the receiver, he thought it over. Eddie sounded sick all right. But something about the conversation puzzled him. Maybe Mark would be a little more specific.

Mark arrived about seven o'clock and managed to attract Soapy's attention on his way back to the stockroom. But Chip learned nothing from the big-little Redding. Mark clammed up completely when Chip tried to find out what was wrong with Eddie. He disappeared immediately after disposing of the malted and banana split which Soapy provided.

Chip couldn't get Eddie out of his mind. By ten-thirty, he was so concerned that he got permission from George Grayson to leave early. He knew he would have to hurry, but he was determined to find out what was really wrong with the boy.

The same crowd of boys were lounging in front of the candy store. However, this time Chip kept going, nodding in the direction of Tony Carlara but caring little whether or not the boy acknowledged the gesture. He could feel the unfriendly eyes boring into his back, and it was all he could do to restrain the impulse to face about and challenge their arrogance. He was glad when he reached the ugly brick house in which Eddie lived.

Eddie's aunt opened the door. "Oh, Mr. Hilton," she said, "come in. I suppose you came to see Eddie. It's awfully nice of you, but he's in bed and I'm afraid he's asleep."

"That's all right, Mrs. Clark," Chip said, stepping inside. "I'm in a hurry to get home and I can't stop, but I thought I'd drop by and see how he was feeling."

Mrs. Clark smiled. "Eddie isn't feeling so bad physically, Mr. Hilton. But his spirits are pretty low. You see, he's completely wrapped up in his job with you at the drugstore and—well, frankly I think that's what caused the trouble."

"Trouble?"

"Argument is probably the correct word. Anyway, Eddie had some sort of an argument or scuffle with one of those boys down on the corner and I guess he got the worst of it."

"You mean he was in a fight?"

"He certainly looks the part. His face is scratched and he has a cut lip and I think he's going to have a black eye in the morning."

"Did he say whom he was fighting with?"

"He wouldn't talk about it, but one of the girls said the boy was older and bigger. She said Mark tried to help Eddie, but some of the other boys held him and he couldn't do anything."

"When did it happen, Mrs. Clark?"

"Right after school. I've tried to keep the boys

away from that crowd on the corner, but it's almost impossible. Eddie and Mark work after school of course, and what little spare time they have is usually spent in study. But those other boys are *always* on that corner. And they always seem to be in some kind of trouble."

"Are you sure they didn't give any hint as to whom Eddie was fighting with, Mrs. Clark?"

"Well, the boys wouldn't tell me anything. But I heard them talking in their room, and from what I could gather, his name is Bucky somebody—"

Chip nodded. "Well, I'll have to hurry along, Mrs. Clark. Tell Eddie to get well and not to worry about the job."

Chip paused on the sidewalk and thought it over. Now he knew. . . . He looked at his watch. Ten minutes to eleven! Ten minutes to make it to Jeff and beat Ralston's curfew. It was going to be close.

Instead of going back to the candy-store corner and turning up Tenth Street, Chip decided to take a short cut and avoid Main Street. He turned left from the battered brick house and set out at a good steady trot. The neighborhood got worse; the houses were more decrepit and the lights seemed dimmer and farther apart. He lengthened his stride. Then he heard the running footsteps, almost in time with his own. But he dismissed the thought. The sound was probably the echo of his own footsteps.

In a few minutes he left the slum area and entered a neighborhood of small houses. There were more pedestrians here, and up ahead he could see the stadium tower. He slowed down and looked at his watch again. Three minutes! Then he heard the running footsteps once more.

Directly ahead, the sidewalk was lined with large

trees. Just as the shadows darkened, Chip ducked behind the trunk of one of the largest of the trees. The runner was closer now and Chip peered around the other side of the tree. It was Soapy! Chip stepped out and caught him around the body in a half-tackle. "What's the idea?" he demanded. "Following me, huh!"

"What d'ya mean?" Soapy blustered. Then he capitulated. "All right, so I was following you! You weren't kiddin' me when you said you'd see me later and slipped out the side door. Mr. Grayson let me off, too. I knew where you were going and the rest was easy. How's Eddie?"

Soapy listened restlessly as Chip repeated his conversation with Mrs. Clark. When Bucky Husta was mentioned, Soapy burned. "I saw the little stinker on the corner," Soapy said disgustedly. "Why, he's twice as big as Eddie! Somebody endowed that squirt with an overdose of low cunning and a barrel of poor sportsmanship."

CHAPTER 9

A SMALL PRICE TO PAY

HENRY ROCKWELL was a player's coach: experienced, thorough, persistent, and patient. As Curly Ralston's chief assistant, he was in charge of the varsity backfield. He was responsible for the split-second timing required in the performance of Ralston's clever, unbalanced-T plays. Rockwell had coached Chip in high school, as an end of two years, and then for two more as the Valley Falls High School varsity quarterback. Chip's wizardry with the ball was the result of hours of patient instruction under Rockwell's supervision while he was playing in high school. Rockwell never made personal references in his criticism; there was never a hint of anger, no heated tones, no ridicule, and no sarcasm when a mistake was made.

State's backfield players enjoyed working with the veteran coach, not only because of his attitude but because he was an expert at making an objective analysis of a mistake and then had the patience to explain, in minute detail, the proper technique.

It was apparent that State's coaching staff was concerned about Southwestern. Victory meant a long step toward conference leadership. Rockwell was sending the backs through Ralston's intricate plays time and again. There was little Rockwell could teach Chip about handling the pigskin. Chip was uncanny in his ability to conceal the ball, fake handoffs to speeding backs, or find the open receiver for a pass. The veteran assistant coach had taught his protégé the proper techniques, but Chip was the only player Rockwell had ever known who could execute the correct moves and add something to them.

Tims Lansing and several other students were in the bleachers watching the practice. Lansing was concentrating on every move Chip made. "He's the greatest!" he said aloud.

"Who's the greatest?" a companion echoed.

"Chip. Chip Hilton, the quarterback with the first string."

"Is he really as good as everyone says?"

"Better!"

"Aw, you're saying that just because you're a good sport. If you hadn't gotten hurt, you would have been the regular quarterback and you know it!"

Lansing shook his head. "Never in a million years. Believe me! I mean it! Watch this!"

Chip took the ball from Brennan, pivoted to the right, and with his left hand seemed to give the ball to Ace Gibbons racing through the right side of the line. Then Chip straightened up, watched Gibbons' progress, and with his right hand behind his back, apparently fed the ball to Fireball Finley cutting to the weak side. Moving lazily back, Chip watched the two ball-carriers as they sped in different directions.

"Fullback has the ball," one of Lansing's companions said confidently.

"Maybe," Lansing said dryly.

At that moment Chip's indolent posture disappeared and his right arm streaked back and up and the ball whirled straight as a string fifty yards upfield. Big Philip Whittemore gathered the spinning sphere on his fingertips without breaking stride.

There was a gasp of surprise from Lansing's companions. "I could have sworn the fullback had the ball!" "I thought Gibbons had it." "He's a magician!"

"See what I mean," Lansing drawled, grinning at the discomfiture of his pals.

Rockwell worked through all the pass series, alternating each one with a take-off running play, and Chip threw passes until he thought his arm would fall off. Rock wasn't satisfied. Gibbons' fake wasn't quick enough, Finley faked too fast, and Morris' fake didn't fool anyone. Then the ends caught it. Whittemore buttonhooked left when he should have turned right. Higgins didn't start fast enough, Schwartz let the tackle slow him down, Curtis gave away the direction he was going to cut by turning his head too soon.

When Burk and McGuire took turns at the quarterback position, nothing clicked. Because of the loss of Tims Lansing, Rockwell had converted the two halfbacks into quarterbacks. His patience with the two boys was unbelievable. Time after time he repeated a play, his clear, modulated voice showing no annoyance, no matter how serious the mistake. It was a long, monotonous, heartbreaking drill.

Ralston worked with the line in much the same fashion, calling the plays and checking the single- and double-team blocking; the timing, the charge, the high and low, the turn, the cross-body, the straight shoulder, the reverse body, the reverse shoulder, the head block, the standing block, and all the others which were part of the repertory of a Ralston lineman.

Chip wasn't the only player who breathed a deep

sigh of relief when Ralston bellowed, "That's all! Three and in!"

A good shower and the brisk use of a towel does a lot for tired muscles. Chip was dead tired when he took off his football gear, but full of pep when he put on his clothes. The jaunt with Soapy, Fireball, and Whitty down to State Drug gradually eased his tight muscles.

On the way, half-listening to the chatter of his companions, Chip caught himself thinking about his conversation with Eddie's aunt. He hadn't thought much about it at the time, but later one remark in particular struck home. He could almost hear her now. "Eddie is completely wrapped up in his job with you at the drugstore, and frankly, I think that's what caused the trouble."

Mark Redding appeared at the drugstore at seven o'clock and reported that Eddie was better. "Eddie's black— Eddie will be back tomorrow, Chip. I guess I'd better take over for him tonight. What do you want me to do first?"

Chip wanted to laugh but Mark's serious expression checked him. "But you don't have working papers, Mark. Mr. Grayson and all of us would get into trouble if we let you work without papers."

"Aw, working papers don't make any difference, Chip. I deliver papers, don't I?"

"Maybe it's different with a newspaper route, Mark. Now, listen. Do you want to do me a big favor?"

"Sure, Chip. Anything!"

"Well, I want to know about the fight. Why did Bucky Husta jump on Eddie?"

Mark's blue eyes opened wide. "How'd you know it was Bucky?"

"I knew."

Marks jaw squared and his eyes narrowed. "I'm gonna beat him up good just as soon as I'm a little bigger. He's nothin' but a bully. Eddie might have got hurt bad if Mr. Caruso hadn't stopped it. Bucky never starts anything when Tony's around. Tony's tough but he fights fair. That's more than you can say about Bucky! He's afraid of Tony."

"What was the fight about?"

Mark hesitated. "It—it was about you, Chip. Eddie had the clipping from the paper—the one with the picture. He was showing it to the guys on the corner and telling them about you and Bucky told him to shut up."

"Then what happened?"

"Well, Bucky said he didn't want to hear any more about college slobs who just played sissy games and couldn't fight or do something real. Then he told Eddie something else and—well, I can't tell you what that was about—and they had a fight. The man in the candy store—that's Mr. Caruso and he's my boss—broke that up, but Eddie got the worst of it all right."

"I should think he would," Chip said. "What can't you tell me, Mark?"

"Well, you see—" A sudden spasm of fear crossed Mark's face. "I can't tell you any more, Chip. You won't tell Eddie I told you about the fight, will you, Chip?"

Chip shook his head. "I won't tell, Mark. Word of honor. Now let's go see Soapy and have some ice cream. Then you'd better go home. Right?"

Later, on the way to Jeff, Chip told Soapy, Whitty, and Fireball what he had learned about Eddie's trouble. Whitty and Fireball were indignant but

Soapy was furious. It was all the others could do to keep him from going back right then to do something about Bucky Husta.

"Dirty sneak!" Soapy fumed. "Jumpin' on a nice little guy like Eddie. What for?" he continued. "Why would Husta want to beat *him* up?"

"I don't believe you got the whole story, Chip," Whittemore observed. "There's something else. Got to be!"

"Sure there is," Fireball agreed.

"Whatever it is," Chip said quietly, "I intend to find out. I think we'll have to be careful not to get Tony and Bucky and the corner crowd completely down on Eddie. We'd better go slow about trying to help Eddie, too. I've only known him a short time, but I think the little guy would like to fight his own battles. Most kids do."

"I'd like to fight just one of his battles," Soapy said. "Just one!"

"It's a shame someone can't do something about that bunch," Chip mused aloud. "It's not right for those kids to be hanging around on that corner at all hours of the day and night."

"No one could do anything with that bunch, Chip," Soapy said hotly.

"We'll see," Chip said softly.

The rest of the journey home was made in silence and each went to bed wishing he could fight Eddie Redding's battles. Eddie would have figured a black eye, a cut lip, and sundry other bruises to body and pride a small price to pay indeed, if he had known the extent of the affection and loyalty his new friends felt toward Mark and himself.

CHAPTER 10

NOW IT'S UP TO THE KIDS

GEORGE GRAYSON was supervising a new window display Wednesday evening when Eddie reported for work. The proprietor's keen eyes took in Eddie's swollen face and the blackened eye, but he said nothing. Later, however, he called Chip to his office. "What happened to your new assistant?" he asked abruptly.

Chip told Mr. Grayson about Eddie's trouble with Bucky Husta and described the interest Soapy and Fireball and Whittemore had taken in the boy. George Grayson smiled broadly when Chip told him of Soapy's efforts to put some meat on the youngster's frame.

"I agree with Soapy," he said, nodding his head. "Someone should fatten him up. Tell Soapy I'll chip in on the cost of those malteds." He reflected a moment, and then continued, "Tell you what, I'll stand the cost of the three malteds each night if Soapy and his fountain crew will stake Eddie to a membership in the 'Y.' All right?"

Chip told Mr. Grayson that it was more than all

right and hurried downstairs to tell Soapy the good news. Then they began to work in earnest with their protégé. Soapy floated Eddie in malteds and the boy gained weight steadily. When the redhead got the youngster on the scales Friday evening, Eddie weighed an even ninety-eight pounds.

"It's a new record," Soapy boasted. "Now for the hundred!"

Chip stuck to his program. He encouraged Eddie in the breathing exercises and utilized every opportunity to teach the boy something about boxing and wrestling. After Soapy weighed Eddie Friday night, Chip grasped his assistant by the arm, ushered him out the front door, and hurried him up Main Street.

"Where we going?" Eddie demanded, lengthening his stride and trying to equal Chip's pace.

"We're going to the Y.M.C.A.," Chip said firmly. "Mr. Grayson's on the board of directors and he wants me to sign you up for a junior membership."

Eddie stopped abruptly. "Uh, uh," he said, pulling back. "I'm not joining any Y."

"But you want to learn boxing and judo, don't you?"

"Yes, but I'm not joining any Y to learn boxing or this here judo, whatever that is—"

"Yes, you are," Chip said. "Come on, only take a minute."

"But I can't afford it," Eddie persisted. "I've got to work."

"It's all paid for," Chip assured him. "Soapy and Fireball and Whitty chipped in for the membership fee, and Mr. Grayson said you could have an hour off every night to attend the classes. O.K.?"

"But none of the guys around my way belong to the Y, Chip. It means troub—"

"Trouble!" Chip echoed. "What do you mean?"

Eddie shook his head and pressed his lips into a thin line. "Nothing," he said in a low voice.

Signing up took only a few minutes and they were ushered down to the big gymnasium. There were two instructors on the job, each surrounded by a small group of boys. One instructor was teaching boxing in a regular ring set in the middle of the gym, and the other was demonstrating judo holds on a wrestling mat in a corner. Eddie's eyes lighted up, and he moved instinctly toward the judo class. Chip followed, jubilant because of Eddie's apparent interest. Fifteen minutes later he was hustling back to State Drug highly pleased with himself.

"How'd you make out?" Soapy asked, when Chip paused at the fountain.

"You should have seen him," Chip said, grinning. "Pitched right in! Last thing I saw was Eddie trying to throw a two-hundred-pound kid over his shoulder."

Eddie showed up bright and early Saturday morning, eager as always to get right to work. Chip was full of thoughts about the game with Southwestern that afternoon but he took time to talk to Eddie about the Y and the judo class. Toward noon, football fever seemed to grip everyone who came in the store. Then the tenseness took its grip on Chip.

"Come on," Chip chided himself. "Cut this out! You'll be a wreck before the game even starts!"

Chip wasn't the only State partisan who was tense. Every football fan in the state knew Southwestern was the big test. Not that anyone expected a miracle. No one game made a season. Not with Cathedral and the Dukes and Midwestern and Wesleyan and A. & M. yet to come. But Southwestern had won the Sugar

Bowl game, and every starter was back. If the kids could make a good showing it would sure help.

Yes, football was in the air and on the tip of every tongue in University. And, naturally, it was all Southwestern. "Outweigh us twenty pounds a man on the line!" "Same thing in the backfield!" "Beat Brandon thirty to nothing!" "They'll run Ralston's sophomores right out of the stadium!" "Remember last year? Remember the trouncing they gave us? It'll be worse this afternoon!" "Don't follow Ralston's reasoning. Trying to play big-time football with a bunch of kids!"

It was impossible for the players to escape all the adulation for Southwestern. They heard "Sugar Bowl Heroes" at every turn; heard Southwestern on the streets and in the restaurants and in the stores and on the radio and television and read about the team's great prowess in every newspaper.

Curly Ralston, Henry Rockwell, and Jim Sullivan caught it, too. They heard all the tributes and read all the raves, but it was old stuff to them and they shrugged it off. It meant nothing to them personally, but that didn't mean they were unworried about the effect on the players. Ralston paced restlessly back and forth in the coaches' office while the team was dressing. Suddenly he turned to Sullivan. "Take a turn through the locker room, Jim," he suggested. "See if you can figure out how they feel."

Ralston and Rockwell sat in silence after Sullivan left, each going over in his own mind all the little things a coach reviews before an important game. A strong friendship had developed between these two men, so much unlike yet so strongly devoted to the same principles. Ralston broke the silence, his worried frown relaxing slightly as he eyed his first assistant. "Think they'll crack, Rock?"

Rockwell shook his head, his thin lips curling slightly upward as he answered. "No," he grunted, "I don't!"

"How about a little talk before the game? Think they need it?"

Again Rockwell shook his head. "No, Curly," he said soberly, "I think we should treat this game just like any other." He paused briefly and then continued, "They're up. Way up. We've done all we can. Now it's up to the kids!"

Sullivan came tramping up the steps from the gym, and the two older men eyed the door expectantly. There was a smile on Jim's face when he opened the door and entered the office. "Somebody is in for a rude awakening," he said lightly, "and it isn't going to be us—" He dropped heavily into a chair beside the desk. "This is the first time in the memory of man that a State team was all suited up and ready to go twenty minutes ahead of time."

"That means they're ready," Ralston said crisply. "And it means you're right, Rock. They're up! Come on. Let's get 'em out on the field before they explode!"

Chip had dressed quickly. Then, aware of the tension which gripped his teammates, he leaned back against the wall and tried to relax—but he couldn't get his thoughts off the game. He nearly jumped out of his uniform when Curly Ralston opened the door and shouted, "Let's go!"

Fifty thousand spectators were in the stadium when State ran down the runway and out on the green sod in their "home" uniforms of spotless white jerseys, red helmets, and blue pants. As the players spread across the field in front of the home bench for their warm-up drills, it seemed to Chip that every person in the place must be cheering for State. Then Southwestern ran out on the field and the roar sounded even more deafening.

Chip was loosening up his kicking leg, and as he warmed up, he studied the Southwestern players. Their orange jerseys and yellow pants made them appear bigger than their reported weights. But big as they were, Chip noted their speed. "Big and fast," he muttered. "This is going to be tough."

Chip was right. The visitors were big, fast, tough —and overconfident. Chip booted the ball into the end zone on the opening kick-off and the ball was brought out to the twenty-yard line. Then the visitors clicked off eighty yards in nine plays to score a touchdown and kick the extra point before the game was five minutes old. State received and advanced to mid-field, but the Southwestern defense tightened and Chip was forced to punt. He angled the ball out of bounds on the Southwestern five-yard stripe, but the visitors swung right into high again and marched to the State thirty before giving up the ball on downs.

Throughout the first half, Southwestern was cocky and careless but could do nothing wrong. State was determined and full of fight but could do nothing right. At the half Southwestern led, 13 to 0.

The tide turned in the second half. State received and Chip caught the ball on his own five-yard line. He saw a glimpse of daylight straight up the middle and was through the hole and on his way before you could say "touchdown." He might have gone all the way, too, except for a poor block by Higgins. Larry left his feet a split second too soon, so the kicker brought Chip down on the Southwestern forty.

Chip passed on the first play, faking to Finley on a draw play and chucking a hard aerial to Higgins on the visitors' fifteen. Larry made it to the ten and it was first and goal for State in the first minute of the second half. Chip carried the ball himself for three fast strides and then pitched out to Finley. Fireball was forced to the side-line but pegged a hard pass to Whittemore crossing over behind the Southwestern safety and Whitty held the ball for the touchdown. Chip kicked the extra point. The score: Southwestern 13, State 7.

Southwestern received and Chip again kicked the ball into the end zone. Then the visitors tried to get the seven points back in a hurry. Held for no gain on two running plays, the quarterback tried a fast pass into the flat, but Speed Morris came from nowhere to snare the ball and speed across the goal line for another touchdown. Chip again kicked the extra point and the big scoreboard showed State ahead, 14 to 13, with only three minutes gone in the second half.

The game turned into a real battle then. Southwestern was scared and turned on the heat, but State fought right back. Then the visitors got a big break. After an exchange of punts the Southwestern quarterback lofted a high, fifty-yard pass which Ace Gibbons deflected all right, but the ball landed smack into the hands of the visitors' right end in the end zone. The try for extra point was good and Southwestern led, 20 to 14.

Lightning does strike twice in the same place and football breaks care nothing about personalities. Mike Brennan elected to receive and the visitors' kicker booted the ball high and long and straight to Ace Gibbons. Ace dropped back a few steps, concentrated on the ball until it stuck in his hands, and then started upfield at full speed. He got off to a fast start and sped across the twenty, the thirty, and up to the forty-yard line before he was hit. Then he fumbled!

Southwestern recovered, faked a line play, and scored on a rifle pass to the same right end. The tall receiver fought with Ace Gibbons for the ball and won the tussle for another touchdown. Gibbons was so angry because of the play that he took himself out of the game. Ralston substituted Junior Roberts and met Ace at the side-line. He tried to console Gibbons, who was in a frenzy. The home fans were stunned by the suddenness of the break but they gave Gibbons an understanding cheer.

Biggie Cohen broke through the line like a mad bull to make the kicker hurry the try for extra point, and the ball flew wide of the goal. But McCarthy was off side and the second try was good. That made the score 27 to 14 and State's hopes dimmed. When the referee gave Mike Brennan his choice, Mike surprised everyone by electing to kick. "Gotta get the ball down in their end of the field someway!" he growled.

Before State could line up for the kick, the quarter ended and the teams changed goals. Chip's kick was high and down to the Southwestern five-yard line, where Finley dropped the receiver before he had taken three steps. The State fans liked the bone-crushing tackle and began to chant "Fight, Team, fight! Fight, Team, fight!"

It may have been the "fight" cheer or the sight of the game clock ticking away State's championship hopes. Whatever it was, it brought results. Tiny Tim McCarthy and Mike Brennan and Soapy Smith and Biggie Cohen and Joe Maxim tore through the Southwestern line and chased the ball carrier across the goal line for a safety. But it was small consolation. The clock showed twelve minutes to play with the score: Southwestern 27, State 16.

Southwestern kicked and Finley carried the ball to the visitors' forty-five. Chip hit Whittemore with a buttonhook pass which was good for ten and a first down, and then Southwestern held three straight times. It was fourth and eight with the ball on the visitors' thirty-three yard line. In the huddle, Chip called for a pass but Brennan overruled him. "Kick, Chip!" Mike urged. "Kick the field goal! I've got a hunch!"

Chip hesitated and Brennan continued. "They're tired, Chip. If you kick it they'll receive and we'll take it away from them again. I've got the feeling. I know we'll do it! Right, gang?"

Chip didn't like it, but he changed the call and State came out of the huddle in place-kick formation. That brought a groan from the State fans and some derisive remarks from the opponents.

"What goes? You guys afraid of a little contact football?"

"Now I've seen everything! Eleven points behind and they try for a field goal!"

"Who's callin' the plays for you guys—the trainer?"

With Speed holding, Chip booted a perfect placement and that made the score: Southwestern 27, State 19. The visitors received, and Mike Gibbons dropped the receiver in his tracks on the Southwestern eight-yard line. His vicious tackle seemed to set the pattern. Three straight times Cohen, McCarthy, and Maxim fought through the visitors' forward line as if it were made of paper, to force the ball back to the four-yard line. That made it fourth and fourteen. Chip beckoned to Speed and backed up to midfield, hoping Speed or he would have a chance to make a good runback. But he got a better break. Biggie crashed through the line and knocked the backfield blocker, the ball, and the kicker in three different directions, giving Silent Joe Maxim the chance to fall on the ball for a touchdown.

The State fans nearly tore down the stadium when

the referee threw his arms overhead to designate the score. And they were still in a frenzy when Chip booted another perfect placement for the extra point. That made the score: Southwestern 27, State 26, with five minutes left to play.

Chip turned after the kick and moved over beside Biggie Cohen. "We've got to have the ball, Biggie," he said. "Remember our old Valley Falls on-side play? I'm going to try it! Tell Whittemore to block their tackle out and you block the guard in. I'll tell Speed. He'll get the ball. O.K.?"

Cohen nodded grimly. "We'll take care of the blocking," he muttered. "You tell Speed he better get that ball!" He turned away but hesitated long enough to say, "Now you're doin' some *real* quarterbacking!"

Mike Brennan was jubilant, clapping his teammates on the back and challenging them to make the kick-off tackle. "We've got 'em back on their heels, now," he exulted. "Let's go get 'em! Let's get that ball! What d'ya say, gang? Give us a high kick, Chip!"

Chip was tempted to tell Mike about the short kick but was afraid of a tip-off to the opponents lining up outside their restraining line. The execution of an on-side kick requires perfect deception; everything, but everything, has to point to a downfield boot. So Chip remained silent, praying he could execute his part accurately and that Speed and Biggie and Whitty would do the rest.

Brennan had his teammates steamed up all right. If it was deception Chip was worried about, they eliminated that item pronto. They charged down the field and through the visitors as if they were sprinting a hundred-yard dash—that is, all but Cohen and Whittemore and Speed Morris. The dashing wave of players fooled Southwestern, the fans, and the officials as well. Suddenly they saw the slithering ball bouncing along the ground past mid-field to the Southwestern's forty-five yard line, right between Cohen and Whittemore. Then they saw two of the best blocks ever thrown in any football game and the way was clear for Speed Morris to dive on the ball and enfold it under his curled-up body.

It took a second for the import of what they had witnessed to dawn upon the fans, but then they were on their feet, programs and hats and coats and blankets flying. The referee was standing over Speed and pointing toward the Southwestern goal. It was State's ball first and ten, on the Southwestern forty-five yard line with four minutes and fifty seconds to play.

Chip's teammates were completely mystified. "What happened?" Brennan demanded. "Bad kick?" He was panting heavily after his mad dash down the field and looked from Chip to Speed and Cohen and Whittemore for the explanation.

"Tell you later," Chip said. "Come on, now. This is our big chance!"

The Southwestern captain was a veteran of many close and tough games and immediately called time. That gave Chip a chance to work up a sequence of plays, and when time was in, his teammates knew exactly what was coming. And they clicked! An over-the-line toss to Higgins was good for five, Fireball hit through the middle for three, and Speed darted over tackle on a quick-opener for three more and the first down. Now it was first and ten on the Southwestern thirty-four-yard line and "We want a touchdown" came booming in toward the two teams from every direction.

Chip darted straight back from the center, faking a hand-off to Fireball driving through the middle, faking another to Speed on the way, and raised the ball as if for a long pass. Just when it seemed the charging visitors would throw him for a loss, he flipped an underhand pass to Whittemore cutting around behind his own line. Whitty broke through a hole inside the Southwestern end and carried to the twenty for another first down. Southwestern called another time-out.

In the huddle, Chip ran through his plans, thankful for the extra time. "We can't risk an interception now, gang," he said. "We'll stick with running plays and try to keep in the center of the field. O.K.?"

Brennan patted Chip on the back. "That's the ticket, Chipper." He looked around the circle of faces. "This is our big break, gang. Chip is figuring on a place-kick if we can't gain. Right, Chip? That means we've got to hold that line if he has to try for the three-pointer." He thrust out his hand. "This is our last chance, gang. Don't boot it!"

Southwestern stiffened, and after three plays, the ball rested on the fifteen-yard line practically in the center of the field. The bedlam was deafening now, but it didn't bother the State players. It wasn't necessary for Chip to call the signals in the huddle. He simply extended his hand and every player joined in the team clasp, each determined to do his job.

While his teammates were in the huddle, Speed moved up to a position six and a half yards behind the ball and carefully stretched a piece of tape along the path he expected Chip's toe to travel. When the team broke out of the huddle and moved up to the ball, Southwestern was already dug in, prepared to charge. There wasn't any question in their minds about the possibility of a kick.

Chip concentrated on the tape and called the signals. On the count of three the ball came spinning back and Speed plopped it down as unconcernedly as if it was merely a practice kick instead of one which meant another long step toward the conference championship. Chip's job was routine. He booted the ball quickly and surely. It whirled end over end and over the goal, splitting the posts for a perfect three-pointer. State led, 29 to 27, with a minute left to play, and the stands erupted like a volcano, spilling fans and spectators down on the running track and out on the side-lines.

Southwestern received and Chip booted the ball clear over the end zone and into the crowd of fans. That left fifty seconds to play and time for Southwestern to try three passes from their own twenty, all of them incomplete. Before the quarterback could get the ball in play for the last desperate pass, the timekeepers gun ended the game and State had won its big game.

CHAPTER 11

SHOWING UP THE EXPERTS

MAIN STREET had been the scene of many a victory parade during the years State had been located in University. But none could equal the unplanned celebration which followed the Southwestern victory. The snake dance had formed on the field right after the game and had made its way downtown. By the time Chip and his teammates reached the business section of the city, Main Street was a boiling mass of frenzied football maniacs.

"You would think we'd won the national championship," Soapy quipped.

State Drug was surrounded but they managed to get through the mob and slip through the side entrance on Tenth Street. Few of the celebrants recognized their football heroes. Soapy lowered a shoulder and did his best blocking of the day as he plowed a path back to the stockroom. Slipping quickly into his fountain coat, Soapy fought his way to the fountain, loudly proclaiming to all and sundry that "business must continue as usual, ladies and gentlemen, irrespective of the limited staff of employees on hand to meet this unusual demand."

The crowd promptly recognized their football

heroes when they appeared in their working coats. Then the commotion reached such proportions that Pop King, who was a special-duty policeman at the corner, ambled in and smilingly threatened to "call the wagon." But the wise old policeman had been through all this many times down through the years. When he saw he was wasting his breath, he made his way to the back of the store where he could get a better view of the proceedings.

Fireball spotted King in the back of the store and seized the opportunity to usher his policeman pal into the stockroom where Chip was talking to Eddie and Mark. "Chip," Fireball interrupted, "this is Pop King." He paused and then continued significantly, "Pop knows Tenth Street inside and out. Well, gotta run. See you later, Pop."

Chip acknowledged the introduction and started to introduce Eddie and Mark, but King checked him. "I know these fellows," King said, ruffling Mark's hair. "They live on my beat. I'm just helping out over here today because of the crowd." He gestured toward Eddie. "How's this young fellow making out on the job?"

"He's doing all right," Chip said warmly. "He's a fine worker."

King studied Chip appreciatively. "You fellows are showing up the experts, aren't you?"

Chip smiled. "I guess we're lucky."

"Not from what I hear," King said.

"Chip won the game," Mark bragged. "I watched it on television."

"Want to do me a favor, Eddie, Mark?" Chip interrupted. "See if you can get me a Sunday paper."

When the youngsters disappeared, Chip turned to King. "Do you have a couple of minutes?"

King laughed. "With that mob out there? I sure do! I'm sittin' right here until they run out of steam. Now you go ahead, young feller. Shoot!"

"I wanted to talk to you about the crowd of kids that hang out on Tenth Street outside the corner candy store. The crowd Eddie and Mark hang around with—"

King shook his head. "Oh, them! That isn't a crowd, that's a gang of young hoodlums. Not the little ones now. Not the little fellers like Mark. And not the followers like Eddie. But the rest of them—well, they're headed in the wrong direction. What's on your mind?"

"Well, Eddie has been having trouble with one or two of the bigger kids and I'd like to help him. The trouble is, I don't know how to go about it."

King nodded understandingly. "I know," he said, "I know. Eddie Redding is a nice kid, but he's been hanging around that corner crowd for the last few months and now he's one of them—like the other kids in that neighborhood."

"But don't their parents try to keep them at home?"

"Son," King said kindly, "the people who live down on those back streets are pretty discouraged. When they reach the stage that they *have* to live in that section, they've just about hit bottom. I've chased that bunch of kids a hundred times. But soon as I turn *my* back—*they're* back! If the parents would cooperate, I might be able to do something. But they won't, or else they haven't time, and the kids are just about out of hand."

"I guess you know Tony Carlara and Bucky Husta."

King nodded grimly. "I know them well enough.

Too well! Not bad kids at heart, at least Tony isn't, but the way they're going, there is only one answer—trouble!"

"They seem to have Eddie scared to death. At least that's the impression I get, and I don't like it. Do you think I can help him in any way? I'd like to help the whole bunch if I could. How about the Police Athletic League? Can't they do anything?"

"Well," King drawled, "yes and no. If we could get a little cooperation from the parents and the kids themselves we could do a lot. So far, we haven't had a bit of luck in that neighborhood.

"Tell you what, Hilton. Why don't you go see Lieutenant Byrnes of the Juvenile Delinquent Division? He's down at 499 Main Street. He's recreational director of the PAL Youth Center and knows most of the answers. Does a fine job. He's a great sports fan and I know he'd be happy to meet you. I'll tell him you're coming down. Well, guess I'd better get back on the job. Let me know how you make out. So long."

Eddie came in with the paper right after Pop King left, and for the first time, Chip noticed his depression. But he was wise enough not to comment until he could get a chance to talk to Mark. His opportunity came when Soapy sent for more syrups and Eddie left to fill the order. Then he turned to Mark. "What's wrong with Eddie now?"

"Bucky jumped him again this morning."

"Why?"

"Because he joined the Y."

"What's wrong with joining the Y?"

"Nothin', I guess, except none of the fellows in our neighborhood go up there."

"What happened?"

"Well, Bucky caught Eddie going home and told

him to stay away from the Y, and Eddie said he wouldn't do it, and they got into another fight. Then Tony came along and broke it up. Then Bucky and Tony had an argument, and Tony asked Bucky if he wanted to make something of it and Bucky backed down."

"*That's* different," Chip observed dryly.

"Lots of things gonna be different," Mark boasted. "Feel my muscle. I'm gonna train at the Y too! I'll take care of that Bucky! Just you wait! I'm gonna get good at that jodo stuff—"

"Judo."

"Well, whatever it is."

"How did Bucky find out about Eddie joining the Y?"

"Tony and Bucky find out about everything," Mark said laconically.

Eddie came back then, and Chip dropped the subject. Later, after the rush outside quieted down, Soapy came back with double malteds for Eddie and Mark, and when these had been stowed away, Chip sent the two boys home.

After work that night, Chip and Soapy and Fireball and Whittemore walked down Tenth Street to Pete's restaurant for a midnight snack. Chip was enjoying the privilege of being able to relax and take his time, secure in the knowledge that there was no eleven-o'clock football curfew to worry about that night. Pete was thrilled to have the State football stars in his "joint," as he called it, and introduced Chip and his pals to every customer in the place. Everyone joined in the football conversation which followed, and when Pop King came in at twelve o'clock, they were still at it.

Soapy was right on the job Sunday morning, rabble-rousing his pals and presenting each with a copy of the *Herald* opened to the sports page. And he made a point of drawing the attention of each sleepy friend—and Chip Hilton in particular—to Bill Bell's story of the game.

"Bell says we're the greatest, Chip," Soapy exulted. "Calls you 'Mister Toe!' Says we're gonna win the conference and that we're a cinch for one of the bowl games. Now what do you think of those pumpkins?

"Oh, yes, says here that one Chip Hilton is gonna make All-Conference and he wouldn't be surprised if he made All-America. Says Chip has his vote right now whether or not we win another game!"

Chip couldn't take it; he dressed hurriedly and started for church. After the services he took a long walk, had lunch at Pete's, where he read the sports pages of the *Herald* word for word, and then went back to Jeff and took a nap. After dinner he hit the books, wrote a letter to his mother, and went to bed at ten o'clock.

Ralston had excused the players who had been in the game against Southwestern from Monday practice, so Chip decided it would be a good time to visit the Police Athletic League Youth Center. He told the officer at the desk that his name was Chip Hilton and that he wanted to see Lieutenant Byrnes.

The stern expression on the man's face disappeared as soon as he heard "Hilton." He smiled broadly and extended his hand. "I'm sure glad to know you, Hilton. Thought I recognized you but I wasn't sure. Come on, the boss will be tickled pink. You get banged up any on Saturday?"

Chip assured the officer he was fine, and then he was in a big office and facing a man built like a fullback who rose to his feet and crushed his fingers in a firm handclasp.

"Sit down, Hilton. Pop King said you'd be around to see me. Now, before we get around to anything else, let's talk a little football. Make yourself comfortable there. You sit down, too, Bill.

"Maybe I don't look it, but I played a little football myself. Yes, sir, right here at Central High School. Right here in University. Played fullback three years. Was All-State the last year. I should have gone to college. Had a lot of scholarship offers. Too smart, though. You know how it is with kids—know it all. I wanted to get a job and get married. Got the job! Got married! I have a couple of fullbacks of my own at home right now! They're going to be better than their old man, too!

"Let's see. You've won four in a row now. Hmm. Guess the only team you've got to worry about now is A. & M. They're tough! Won—let's see—thirteen in a row. I'm going to see that game! Going to take the wife! Kids, too!

"Now, let's see. Pop King said you wanted to do something about a corner crowd down on Tenth below Main. Right? Now, how can I help?"

Chip told Byrnes about Tony and Bucky and the difficulty Eddie apparently was having with the corner crowd. "Pop tells me Eddie is a good kid, Lieutenant, and I'd like to help him. Trouble is, I don't know how to go about it.

"I'm familiar with the neighborhood all right. Pop King knows it better than anyone else, of course. Anyway, it's a typical tenement section with the inevitable corner candy store and the corner crowd. Most of the kids are all right but they're at an impressionable age, easily led, and apt to get into trouble if the leadership is bad."

"I don't believe the leadership is too good."

"It seldom is, Hilton. We've been trying to get a toehold in that neighborhood for years. Most of our difficulty has been caused by the constant moving in and out. The only people who dig their roots in down there are the down-and-outers who can't afford to live in a better neighborhood. In most neighborhoods, we can find men and women who are glad to help out with the problem. Down there, they're discouraged and broke and too busy scrambling to make a living to care much about anything."

"Don't the kids themselves want something better?"

"That's hard to answer. Most kids from that sort of a neighborhood run pretty much according to form. They're about all the same. Read a lot of cheap newsstand stuff and try to imitate the villain because he represents someone who flaunts authority.

"The leader is usually a strong, aggressive kid who can lick anyone else in the bunch, or else he's a little smarter and has more leadership. The whole deal is based on each kid's hope of being a member of a gang for personal protection—and, in the case of the boss kid, it's self-esteem. He wants to be feared, envied, and able to bully others."

"That description sure fits Tony and Bucky," Chip was thinking.

"Now," Byrnes continued, "that sort of thing spreads through the whole bunch and all the kids in the neighborhood. The individual members of the group feel strong because they're members of a gang or a club or some kind of a secret society or whatever you want to call it."

"Don't they like sports?"

"Of course. But the big thing with these corner gangs is personal strength or the ability to fight. The one person they respect and admire most is the rough-and-tough alley fighter. That's why they worship punch-drunk fighters and bullies."

Chip was thinking if he could only show them—prove to them that you didn't have to be a bully and a braggart to be a good fighter.

Byrnes had paused and now measured his words carefully as he continued, "Neighborhoods like that one down there on Tenth Street spawn the juvenile delinquent. There you will find the cheap tavern keeper or liquor dealer and the shoddy beer joints. And it isn't only the kids from the poor sections who frequent these joints. Quite often—too often—it's the favorite stamping ground for kids from the other side of the tracks. Kids from the better homes. They can visit these areas without much fear that they will run into their parents or friends of the family. That's where they get their start towards trouble."

"Can't the police do something about the kids hanging around the corners all evening?"

"We—and I mean the police—have tried to get a curfew law in this town for years. But we've never had any luck. It will probably surprise you, but most of the opposition comes from the parents themselves. Not from the middle or wealthier groups, of course, or maybe I'm not right there, either. Anyway, I guess most of the voting parents are afraid that they'll have to stay home and take care of the kids if we run them off the streets.

"That's hard to believe, I know, but it's the truth. Every time it's been brought up for a vote, it's been knocked down. You figure it out."

CHAPTER 12

MALTEDS AND BLACK EYES

CHIP learned a great deal about the aims and objectives of the Police Athletic League from Lieutenant Byrnes, and he learned a lot about the difficulties everyone experiences in attempting to help impressionable youngsters with their vital teen-age problems. But he hadn't found the answer to Eddie Redding's problem, and when he reached State Drug, he ran smack into it again. Eddie was standing on the scales, his whole attitude expressing defeat, while Soapy worked at the weights. Chip paused in the door.

"What goes?" Soapy demanded, slapping Eddie on the back.

"I haven't been eating too much," Eddie said weakly, his voice barely audible.

"But you've only gained two pounds," Soapy said, ruffling Eddie's hair. "Come on," he urged. "Let's get that chin up and get on the ball. Let's see, it's eight o'clock. We'll have three more malteds. You hear! If we're going to make an athlete out of you, we've all got to work together. You have to do your part, too." He looked up and saw Chip. "Eddie's down again, Chip," he said. "Way down."

"He'll snap out of it," Chip said casually. "Don't worry about Eddie."

Soapy went back to his fountain job and Chip and Eddie worked on the stockroom inventory. While they worked, Chip tried to draw him out. But Eddie wasn't talking, and Chip gave up and concentrated on the job. But his concentration was interrupted. Soapy opened the door and ushered Mark Redding through the door.

"Look, Chip, look at this!" Soapy said, pointing to Mark's eye. "Look at Mark's shiner!"

Mark had a beauty. His eye was black above, on the lids, below and half-way down his cheek.

"What happened to you?" Chip gasped.

"Must run in the family," Soapy quipped.

"Don't run in the family," Mark said ominously. "Just wait! Wait until I learn that jodo!"

"Judo," Chip corrected.

Mark measured Chip speculatively. "Judo," he repeated carefully. "Well," he said, "we going to talk or work?"

"Eddie and I are going to work," Chip said decisively. "You're going to do some reading. Right over there at that desk. Here's a book. Now get busy!"

Soapy couldn't understand it. He came back to the stockroom repeatedly, bringing an ice-cream cone for Mark, a malted for Eddie, or a soda for Chip. But it was of no avail. Chip wasn't talking and he wouldn't let Eddie or Mark talk.

On the way home after work, Soapy could restrain his curiosity no longer. "How did Mark get the black eye?" he asked.

"I don't know."

"Don't know," Soapy repeated. "Didn't you ask?"

"No, Soapy, I didn't."

Soapy began grumbling about that being no way to help a kid who needed help and he was surprised by some people's attitude and that it didn't seem possible that a fellow's best friend would be so mysterious about something in which they were both so much interested. Chip let him continue, but just before they reached Jeff, he explained that he felt the best way to help Eddie at the present time was to sit tight and see if the boy could work his way out of his troubles on his own. "Let's wait and see what happens, Soapy. In the meantime I've got to work out a plan—some sort of a campaign—so I can win over that corner crowd."

The days passed and Chip was no closer to a solution. Eddie was still depressed, but every night he and Mark lit out for the Y at seven o'clock for "jodo." All that week University buzzed with football talk; the conference championship, the Rose Bowl, Sugar Bowl, Cotton Bowl, Orange Bowl, and all the others.

Friday came, and just before Chip started for the station to catch the 11:45 P.M. sleeper for the Cathedral game, Soapy weighed Eddie.

"Chip! A hundred and three pounds! A heavyweight!"

The railroad station was jammed. Students, townspeople, professors, fans, and players were crowded on the platform, cheering, yelling, and demonstrating by their enthusiasm that they were behind State all the way. The members of the band were spread all over the platform, hopelessly mixed up with the fans, but playing away for all they were worth. It was irrepressible enthusiasm at its greatest intensity. But when the train pulled out, State's varsity was aboard, every player thrilled by the send-off, determined to justify the fans' faith the next afternoon against Cathedral. And they did!

State won the game in the first ten minutes of the game. Cathedral won the toss, received, and fumbled on the second play. So it was State's ball on the Cathedral thirty and they scored on the first play, Chip zipping a high pass to Higgins in the end zone for the tally. He kicked the extra point and State led, 7 to 0.

Cathedral received again, carried to the twenty-five, and when they couldn't gain were forced to punt. Chip took the kick on the State forty-five and brought it back to the Cathedral forty. Then he used his hidden-ball faking ability and sent Morris streaking through left tackle and all the way across the goal-line. It was as easy as that, and Ralston began substituting. Chip's scoring was limited to four extra points and a twenty-yard field goal. The final score was: State 31, Cathedral 14.

That night they were honored with a steak dinner, each player being the personal guest of a Cathedral player at the country club. Later in the evening they were introduced individually at the big football dance. It was sportsmanship at its best.

On the midnight sleeper, heading back to University, they learned that A. & M. had won its fourteenth straight from Riordon, 39 to 6. But they forgot that when the train rolled into University. It seemed to Chip that the band and the fans must have waited right there all night. This time, however, there was a little more organization. Six baggage trucks were lined up, and the fans wouldn't let the coaches and players leave until each mounted the trucks and took a bow.

Ralston spoke briefly, remarking that a good team

never looked over its shoulder and that one victory or five victories didn't make a season. "We are meeting the Dukes next Saturday. One of the best, if not the best team in the country, and we'll have to work hard. However, since everyone got in the game yesterday afternoon, there will be no practice tomorrow!"

Chip spent that afternoon almost as he did every Sunday, taking a walk to limber up, writing home, and studying. The next afternoon, he had lunch with Tims Lansing and then spent three hours in the library doing research for an English paper. When he got to State Drug, Lieutenant Byrnes was chatting with the unattainable light of Soapy's life, Mitzi Savrill, State Drug's beautiful cashier.

"Hello, Hilton. Nice win! Tough one coming up Saturday, eh?"

"Everyone says they're good, Mr. Byrnes."

"You'll take 'em," Byrnes said confidently. "Is there a place where we can talk? Got time?"

"Sure have," Chip said, smiling at Mitzi. "Come on back to my office."

Back in the stockroom, Byrnes made himself comfortable in the desk chair. "How's your protégé working out?"

"Fine, on the job."

"What kind of a boy is he?"

"Eddie's a good kid, Mr. Byrnes. A fine boy."

Byrnes nodded. "Yes, they're all good kids until they get mixed up with some wise bird who talks them into a lot of trouble. It's the same old story of the company a boy keeps; the one bad apple in the barrel."

"Eddie isn't going to be led into trouble, but he

might be bullied into doing something he doesn't want to do. I'd like to make friends with the kids on that corner, but they're not very receptive."

"You're no exception," Byrnes said dryly. "This town is like all college towns, Hilton. And the kids here in University are like all college-town kids. Most of them are from poor families and from the worse than poor families and they resent you fellows who ride around in cars and taxis and go to college and have nice clothes and lots of spending money."

"You're not talking about me," Chip remonstrated, smiling ruefully. "Nor any of the fellows I know. We're all working our way through school."

Byrnes nodded. "I know. But the kids I'm talking about don't know that. Now back to the kids:

"They're jealous. There isn't a college town in the country where you don't find resentment among the home-town kids toward the college students.

"We've never had any success whatever in organizing a PAL team or group in that neighborhood." He shrugged wryly. "Right where we need it most. Tell you what, suppose I ask Pop King to come in. Saw him heading for his beat down Tenth Street just a few minutes ago and told him to stick around until I saw you. Got time to talk a little longer?"

"I sure have and I sure appreciate your help."

"Kids are my business, Hilton. I'll be right back."

A few minutes later, Byrnes returned with King. "Pop, we've been talking about the kids on Tenth. Hilton says you know about it."

King nodded. "I know about it, all right. I've hoofed that beat for thirty years and I guess I know every man, woman, and kid down there. And I know those kids you're talking about. They're tough."

King waved a hand deprecatingly. "Now, don't

get me wrong. I don't mean they're dead-end kids. But they're wide open for bad influences. One thing is sure, Tony and Bucky will be duck soup for the first tough who comes along. Right now, they're beginning to show dislike for authority and discipline and anyone or anything which represents it. They've got every kid in the neighborhood buffaloed."

"Do you think they've got some kind of hold on Eddie?"

King grinned grimly. "They've got a hold on every kid in that section, Hilton. You probably got this Eddie kid in trouble with Tony and Bucky just because you went to see him. They've got no use for college boys and they won't hold for a kid from their neighborhood having anything to do with their pet hates."

"But we work together!"

"Means nothing. You're still a college student. They probably beat him up Sunday five minutes after you left him."

"But why doesn't he tell someone? You or me or his father?"

King grimaced. "Tell someone? You mean snitch? Why, you've got as much chance of getting one of those kids to talk as that chair. Forget *that!*"

"What about school? And teams, and parties, and things like that?"

"Don't mean a thing to those kids. They're just waiting until they're old enough to quit school and go to work, or maybe hang around some poolroom and eventually get into trouble.

"Kids like that read gangster stories and see every one of those killer-diller pictures that come along. Then, someday a real tough, or some older guy who thinks he's tough, comes along, and they fall for his line and he takes over and then there's real trouble."

"But there must be *something* they like," Chip said. "How about sports? Couldn't they get the kids to playing baseball and basketball?"

Byrnes answered that question. "We've tried to organize teams down there time and again but never had any luck. If we had a community house or a center of some kind in that neighborhood it would help. But the whole area is condemned and that's out."

"How about the Y.M.C.A.?"

Byrnes deliberated. "That's a tough one. For one thing, a lot of the kids don't have the membership fee. Then, too, some of them live too far away. Others just aren't interested."

Lieutenant Byrnes and Pop King departed a little later and left Chip mixed up and discouraged. If Byrnes and King didn't know the answer, there wasn't much chance for him to solve Eddie Redding's problem. If he could only do something to change Tony Carlara and Bucky Husta. . . .

His thoughts were interrupted by a knock on the door. It was Mitzi Savrill. Mitzi was embarrassed. "Chip," she said timidly, "will you do me a big favor?" Without waiting for an answer she plunged on, speaking hurriedly, "I guess everyone is asking you to get tickets for them, but honest, Chip, I've tried to get them everywhere."

Chip smiled. "You want tickets! You'll get tickets! How many?"

"I—I want an awful lot—"

"How many?" Chip interrupted.

"Well, I have my own, of course, but if I could get three more—"

"You'll have them. That's one advantage of making

varsity. We get five complimentary tickets and we can reserve ten tickets for every game. We have to pay for the regular tickets, of course, with the demand the way it is."

"I have the money right here. Gosh, Chip, this is a real favor."

Chip made a notation of the amount and the kind of tickets. And right then he had an inspiration. This was it! Now he had the answer. At least a start toward it. He'd try to win over Tony and Bucky and some of the others with tickets to the football games! Soapy and Fireball and Biggie and Red and Speed and Whitty weren't using all their passes and they would be glad to let him have them if it would help Eddie and Mark.

That evening Eddie was a little brighter. Soapy got him on the scales and he weighed in at a hundred and five pounds. At the first opportunity, Chip broached his ticket idea. "Do you think Tony and Bucky and some of the other fellows in your neighborhood would like to see the game with the Dukes on Saturday, Eddie?"

Eddie shook his head. "Gee—er, Chip, I don't know. I don't think so."

"You and Mark are going, aren't you?" Chip demanded.

"Yes," Eddie said reluctantly. "Mark wants to go awful bad."

"How about Tony and Bucky? Do you want to ask them to go?"

Eddie's indecisive attitude was enough for Chip. "Never mind," he said understandingly. "I'll ask them myself."

CHAPTER 13

IT'S BIG-TIME FOOTBALL

CHIP was really raring to go when he reported for practice Tuesday afternoon. Everything seemed to be working out the way he wanted it. He had purchased the tickets for Mitzi, and he had accumulated enough player complimentary tickets from his pals to accommodate Tony and Bucky and the corner crowd. Chip's teammates were up, too. Every player on the squad seemed anxious to get going, with the result that it was a practice session which brought smiles to the coaches.

It was a fast workout and Ralston was pleased. He sent them to the showers and was waiting when they assembled in the lecture hall. "Nice going, men," he said, nodding his head. "That kind of a workout warms a man's heart. Now, I want to turn this meeting over to Jim Sullivan. Jim knows more about the Dukes than the whole Duke coaching staff. O.K., Jim, it's all yours."

Sullivan spoke with authority, showing that he knew exactly what he was talking about. He diagrammed the Dukes formation, the spacing of the line and the backs; discussed their plays, the outstanding runners, passers, receivers; and then shifted to the defense.

"Their line is terrific," Sullivan emphasized. "If you fellows thought Southwestern had a tough forward line, wait until you see the Dukes. It's the hardest-charging offensive or defensive line I've ever seen. They're bigger, tougher, and smarter than the Southwestern forwards. Defensively, however, they're built to order for trap plays. Their constant charging should set them up perfectly for our trap series. Coach and Rock will talk over the plays they've worked up, so I won't spend any more time on that phase of it. I might add right here that they give the passer a tough time. They bust through the line and swarm all over him to get him to hurry his passes.

"The Dukes secondary uses a combination man-to-man and zone defense against passes. The defensive quarterback tries to mix you up on your blocking assignments by shifting their defensive alignment at the last possible second. Actually, the defense is a standard 6–2–2–1, shifting into a 5–3–3 when a pass seems imminent.

"My scouting charts show the outside backers taking the flat and picking up the ends if they move latterly. Otherwise, these outside backers play zone and help out against the short passes. The wing backs take the ends every time they cut downfield and stay with them until the ball is in the air. The middle backer-up drops back into the slot and plays zone until a receiver enters the area. Then he plays him man to man. If any particular zone is flooded with receivers, the safety man backs it up. He doesn't commit himself until the ball is in the air. I noticed that the weak-side end often dropped back and covered his respective flat zone when the passer ran toward the opposite side. If there was no receiver in the flat, he usually dropped straight back into the secondary. Maybe I can present it a little better on the blackboard. All right, Coach?"

Ralston nodded and Sullivan chalked in the Dukes defense, setting it up against State's unbalanced-T formation. He outlined the standard 6–2–2–1 defense first and then described the shift into the 5–3–3 pass defense. Then he again discussed the Dukes' offense.

"On the offense, as I said before, the line charges hard and fast, which I guess is the reason their ground game is so strong. But they can and will take to the air as a surprise measure. The fullback, Number 45, is their best runner and best passer. He does most of the throwing. The next best runner is Tex Wheat, Number 48. He's the second best passer, too. Well, I guess that's it, Coach."

Ralston took charge and outlined some of the plays which he thought would work against the hard-charging Dukes. Then he excused them with a strong warning to observe the eleven-o'clock curfew.

After work that night, Chip walked as far as Pete's restaurant with his pals. Then he told them that he would meet them later. "Got a little personal business," he said. "Be back in fifteen minutes."

"You're wasting your time," Finley observed, "but we're with you. Good luck!"

The others went into the restaurant but Soapy stood by the door and watched Chip all the way down the street. When Chip was nearly out of sight, Soapy crossed over to the other side and followed slowly.

Chip fingered the tickets in his pocket as he walked along trying to figure how best to approach Tony and Bucky. As he drew near the candy store he could see the crowd on the corner. It was easy to spot Tony's square figure and Bucky's lanky outline. The two leaders and a crowd of lesser and younger fry were engaged in an argument, gesticulating and talking loudly in boisterous voices. But Tony's quick eyes caught and identified the approaching figure. He muttered something and the group quieted.

"Hi, Tony. Hi, fellows," Chip said, slowing his pace.

Tony eyed Chip warily and impersonally, but he made no effort to acknowledge the greeting. His companions waited tensely, waited as if these two were boxers sparring for an opening.

"Long time no see," Chip said, his voice calm and sure. "Thought you might drop into the store."

When Tony remained silent, Chip continued, "Anyway," he said casually, "I've got some tickets for the game Saturday and I thought you might want to see it."

"Game?" Tony repeated slowly. "What game?"

"This Saturday. The game with the Dukes!"

"Never heard of 'em," Tony said slowly. "What kind of a game they play?"

"Football!" someone behind Chip exploded. "Big-time football!"

Tony swung swiftly around. "Who asked you?" he snarled.

Bucky Husta moved in back of Chip and in the direction of the speaker. "Yeah," he echoed, "who asked you?"

There was a sudden, tense stillness and then Chip heard the muffled sound of a body blow. For one brief second Chip was tempted to turn on Bucky. His blood boiled and he would have been unable to control his anger if Bucky had carried the matter

"I've got some tickets for the game Saturday."

further, but nothing happened and Chip concentrated on Tony.

"That's right," he said, "football! The Dukes have one of the best teams in the country. Why, you can't buy a seat for love or money. I'd like you fellows to go as my guests. What do you say?"

Tony took his time about answering and Chip continued quickly, "They're side-line seats, Tony. The best in the stadium!"

For a moment Chip thought Tony was going to accept the offer. But after a brief pause, the lips tightened again and Tony shook his head. "Nah," he said shortly. "We ain't interested in college football. Right, guys?"

The boys backed him up but the response wasn't too enthusiastic. Chip gave it another try. "Suppose I give the tickets to Eddie. Then if you change your mind, he'll have them for you. O.K.?"

Tony shrugged. "Suit yourself," he said.

"Well, I hope you come," Chip said, turning away. "I know the seats and I'll stop to say hello."

"Don't bother," Bucky said nastily. "We won't be there!"

Chip said good night and walked away, completely disgusted because of his inability to click with Tony and his corner pals. "They're impossible," he told himself.

It was ten minutes to eleven when Chip reached Pete's restaurant and his pals were waiting impatiently on the curb.

"Come on," Soapy urged, "we're late." Then he noted Chip's preoccupation. "No luck, eh? I knew it. You're wastin' your time."

"I'll say you are," Whittemore added. "Forget 'em!"

"I can't forget Eddie," Chip remonstrated. "Nor Mark."

"But you've done everything you could," Fireball said. "If the PAL can't handle that bunch, I don't see how you figure you're going to do it."

"Look, Chip," Soapy pleaded. "Let Eddie take care of his own trouble. Gosh, he's been living down there two or three years and nothing serious ever happened."

"That's just it," Chip agreed. "He never had any trouble until I gave him the job."

"But that was doing him a favor," Fireball said.

"Oh, sure," Chip said. "It was a favor, all right." He considered a bit and then continued, "One thing is sure! I'm not going to walk out on him. And," he added grimly, "I'm going to find out just what makes Tony Carlara and Bucky Husta tick!"

"You'd better forget about the Reddings and start worrying about the Dukes," Finley said pointedly. "Better figure out before Saturday just what makes *them* tick!"

Chip had a lot more help determining what made the Dukes tick than he had in deciding what generated Tony Carlara and Bucky Husta. Curly Ralston, Henry Rockwell, and Jim Sullivan talked about nothing but the Dukes; repeating again and again the little scouting tips dealing with false moves, individual player weaknesses and strengths, and the special attacks and defenses they had planned. The previous raves concerning Southwestern were nothing compared to the general reaction regarding the mighty Dukes.

Chip succeeded in getting Eddie to take the football tickets that night after explaining that he had talked with Tony. "If you can get him to take the tickets, Eddie, it's all right. And if you can't, it's all right. O.K.? At any rate, there's two for you and Mark and enough for any of your other friends."

Right afterwards, Soapy came bustling in, all excited. Chip waited patiently for his pal to spring the news. It came when Soapy got Eddie on the scales.

"Look, Chip, a hundred and twelve pounds! Another thing! Saturday morning at eleven o'clock Eddie's going to put on a judo exhibition at the Y!"

"Wonderful," Chip said. "That means he's got to have plenty of sleep. Give him a couple of malteds and send him home. We'll do the same tomorrow night."

Eddie lingered a moment. "Er—Chip, would you go with me Saturday?"

"We'll all go!" Soapy said gleefully. "We'll be your seconds! Right, Chip?"

"Right!" Chip agreed. "We've got to back up the champion. Sure we'll go. Now you get out of here and get to bed."

Coach Ralston let them off light Friday, and everything was set for the mighty Dukes. Chip sent Eddie home full of malteds and sat down at his desk to jot down idly his quarterback instructions. He was completely engrossed in the notes when he heard the sound of running footsteps and Mark came rushing through the door, panting heavily. A sigh of relief escaped his lips when he saw Chip. "Trouble!" he gasped. "Eddie's in trouble! You gotta help!"

Soapy was on Mark's heels, his red hair tousled and his voice angry. "What you doin' out this time of night? It's ten-thirty!"

Mark ignored Soapy and pulled at Chip's arm. "C'mon," he urged. "I'll tell you on the way."

"All right, I'm coming," Chip said uncertainly, glancing at the clock. "But we'll have to hurry. I've got to get home before eleven o'clock or I'll be in trouble." He turned to Soapy. "I'll have to run. See you at the dorm."

Chip and Mark raced out the Tenth Street door, leaving Soapy bewildered by their hurried exit. But only for a second. "Oh, sure!" he muttered, charging toward the fountain.

Mark trotted along at Chip's side, his breath coming in heavy gasps, more from excitement than fatigue. "Eddie's taking a truck!" he exploded. "Mr. Caruso's truck! Eddie and Tony and Bucky!"

"What for? Who's Mr. Caruso? Where are they taking the truck?"

"Mr. Caruso owns the candy store," Mark explained impatiently. "He hauls the papers in the truck for all the newspaper routes. He owns 'em! He's my boss! They're gonna take the truck as soon as he closes the store."

"Where? What for?"

"All I know is Rip and Skids told 'em—" Mark suddenly clapped his hand over his mouth and dropped his head.

"Rip and Skids?" Chip asked gently. "Who are they, Mark?"

But Mark was through talking. At least about Rip and Skids. He ignored the question and pulled Chip into the dark entrance of a building. "We'd better wait here," he whispered. Then he pointed to a dark alley next to the candy store. "Down there," he whispered excitedly. "That's where Mr. Caruso keeps the truck. Right beside the basement door. See, he's turning the lights out right now!" He stopped abruptly. "I guess I'd better go home," he said, his voice barely audible. Then he grasped Chip's arm. "Try to help Eddie, Chip, please." Then he turned and fled.

CHAPTER 14

FOOTBALL ON YOUR HEAD

CHIP waited uncertainly in the dark, watching Caruso turn out the lights. Then the little man banged the front door, tried the knob, and hurried swiftly away in the opposite direction. One light remained burning on the inside of the store. Somewhere, far away, Chip heard the muffled tones of a bell tolling eleven o'clock. "Now, I'm really in the soup," he muttered.

A slight sound drew his attention. A small figure appeared beside the corner of the store and peered up and down the street. Chip recognized Eddie even in the shadowy darkness. Then a sudden thought struck home. Why wasn't Eddie home and where were all the kids? Pop King had said that even when he chased them, they came back and seldom broke up until midnight. And where was Pop King? . . .

Then he heard a starter crank an engine. Backfire, deafening in the black stillness, made him jump. The motor sputtered and died away and the starter whined again. Then Chip went into action. He was committed now, whether it was a trap or the real thing. He dashed down the alley, just as the engine

"As he ran in front of the truck, the twin headlights pierced the darkness."

caught and roared. As he ran in front of the truck, the twin headlights pierced the darkness and, for a brief second, caught him in the blinding glare.

Before the driver could mesh the gears, Chip was on the running board. He tore open the door and snatched the key out of the lock, pressing the weight of his back hard against the boy behind the wheel. Then he turned off the lights and pulled Tony Carlara out on the ground and around in front of the truck.

There was a sudden scurrying on the other side of the seat and two figures sprang to the ground. But they didn't get far. Someone tore alongside at that instant and collared Eddie and Bucky Husta and pulled them forward, crying fiercely, "Oh, no, you don't!" It was Soapy.

"Where did you come from?" Chip demanded, holding Tony firmly by the collar. "I thought you went home."

"Without you!" Soapy grunted. "Huh!" Then he yanked his two prisoners forward. "Now what?" he asked.

"We send Eddie home," Chip said grimly. "And then we walk Tony and Bucky up to the corner for a little talk. Beat it, Eddie. I'll see you at work in the morning."

"Fine thing," Soapy said disgustedly, shaking Eddie roughly. "We let you off so you can get some rest and this is the thanks—" He shoved Eddie, and the little guy took off like Fireball Finley on a line buck.

Chip grasped Tony by the arm and started up the alley toward Tenth Street. Soapy followed with Bucky. Suddenly Bucky tore loose from Soapy's grasp and dashed back down the alley. "You're not takin' me anywhere," he snarled.

"Let him go, Soapy," Chip called, tightening his grasp on Tony. "Tony was driving the truck."

Chip stopped on the corner and backed Tony up against the candy-store window. "Now," he said, holding the truck key in front of Tony's nose, "where did you get this?"

Tony wasn't talking. He pressed his lips together and glared sullenly at the ground. Chip replaced the key in his pocket and grasped Tony by the arm again. "All right," he said firmly, "we'll just take you home and call Pop King and let you explain to him."

That did it. The words spilled out, tumbling one over the other. "You can't do that!" Tony cried. "I wouldn't even get in the door! The old man would go crazy!"

"Then talk! Tell me where you got the key and what you were doing in that truck."

"Caruso hides it—"

"*Mr.* Caruso!"

"Mr. Caruso hides it under the seat. All the guys know that!"

"Is this the first time you tried to take it?"

Tony nodded, his eyes downcast. "Yes," he said, "it's the first time."

"Where were you going with the truck?"

Tony shrugged. "For a ride."

"Did you realize that you were *stealing* the truck?"

Tony shook his head. "We were going to bring it back," he said lamely.

"It's still stealing, isn't it? Suppose you ran into a car or hit someone?"

"Yeah," Soapy added fiercely. "Suppose you killed someone? Think what would happen to you and Eddie and Bucky Husta. And how about your family!"

"I guess I wasn't thinkin' much," Tony said in a low voice, clearing his throat.

"Where does Mr. Caruso live?" Chip asked.

"Just down the block," Tony said hoarsely. "What are you gonna do?"

"We're going to take the key down to his house and tell him what happened," Chip said. Then he added, "And you're going with us!"

"But—"

"No buts! It's that or else!"

"But he don't like me! He'll call the cops!"

"That's a chance we have to take. Come on," Chip said gently. "I don't think he will be unreasonable. After all, the truck wasn't moved. Don't worry. I'll do the talking."

The Caruso family lived on the first floor of a ramshackle brick house. When Chip knocked, the store owner himself cautiously opened the door. "Yes," he said warily, "what is it?"

"Mr. Caruso?" Chip queried.

The little man nodded. "That's me, Frank Caruso." Then he recognized Carlara. "Tony! What's the matter?"

Chip answered the question, handing him the truck key and explaining that Tony had shown them where he lived and that the purpose of the call was to return the key to his truck.

Frank Caruso didn't understand. "This my key?" he demanded. "What's the matter with my truck?"

Chip advised him as clearly as he could that he had surprised some boys in the truck in the alley and had chased them away and thought it best to bring the key to the house. "They evidently knew where you kept the key and might have gotten into trouble. Maybe you ought to carry it with you."

Caruso nodded. "Ah, those boys on the corner. Always they make for me trouble!" He nodded grimly toward Tony. "Him too! Thanks, Mister. You like come in? You like some wine?"

Chip declined the friendly invitation and said good night, and the three boys, Tony in the middle, walked back up the street. Chip half-expected Tony to dash away, but the square-shouldered young leader walked passively along, deep in thought.

Halting on the corner by the candy store, Chip gently shook Tony's shoulder. "That wasn't so bad, was it?"

Tony shook his head. "No, but why didn't you tell him about me? Why didn't you tell him I had the key?"

"Because I think that you're smart enough to realize this sort of thing is going to end up only one way—in serious trouble, jail, reform school, disgrace." After a short pause, Chip continued, "And, Tony," he said pointedly, "because I have confidence in your strength. I know you're strong enough to do your own thinking and stand on your own feet. Strong enough to resist the leadership of fellows who want to use you for dirty work. Fellows like—" Chip paused a long second and then continued—"fellows like Rip and Skids, for instance. Good night, Tony."

Tony's mouth slacked open in surprise. Long after Chip and Soapy had disappeared up Tenth Street, he stood on the corner by the candy store, his hands balled into two hard fists. Then he slowly crossed the street and made his way up the steps leading to the little house on the corner and slipped softly through the front door.

As soon as they were out of Tony's sight, and almost as if by a charging signal, Chip and Soapy broke into a trot. "Boy, I hope Ralston doesn't hear about this," Soapy said. "Must be eleven-thirty."

"I'm not worrying about him hearing about it," Chip said. "I'm going to tell him."

"Tell him? You crazy? He'll throw us off the squad!" When Chip made no reply, Soapy continued pleadingly, "Shakes, Chip, we haven't done anything wrong. It was just the opposite. Heck, you were doing a good *deed*."

"Just the same we broke the rules."

Soapy knew that tone of voice and dropped the subject. They continued on in silence, matching strides, and made Jeff without incident. But as they started up the steps to the second floor, they met Pete Randolph coming down. Soapy grinned, gave the building superintendent his best smile, and said good night, but Randolph merely grunted.

"He's sore," Soapy muttered. "Everybody in this town is so football crazy they think you're insane if you don't walk around with a football on your head."

"All the more reason to tell Coach," Chip said quietly.

Chip wasted no time undressing and getting to sleep, but Soapy kept muttering about the injustice of being an athlete and trying to serve two masters and why wasn't the curfew twelve o'clock for fellows who had to work nights to get through college.

Saturdays were big days for the businessmen of University. The students were free from classes and descended upon the stores and shops like a tidal wave. Not that the proprietors minded. Far from it. But this morning when Chip hurried along Main Street it wasn't business that occupied the minds of the owners and employees and the early customers. It was football! Nothing but football! And there were

State flags and decorations and painted signs on the windows and on the street and sidewalks. Chip was becoming a public figure now, and more than one person waved a friendly hello to the tall youngster with the yellow hair and long strides.

When Chip reached State Drug, he found Eddie waiting in the stockroom. Eddie's eyes were downcast, his whole manner subdued. Chip said good morning and sat down at the desk, keenly aware that Eddie was under a terrific strain. Finally, Eddie broke and walked over to the desk. "I'm sorry, Chip," he said tremulously. "I *had* to do it."

Eddie's remorse was obvious and all of Chip's sympathies were aroused. But he was determined to get to the bottom of the affair. "*Why* did you have to do it, Eddie?" he asked.

"Well, I didn't want to do it. But Tony and Bucky said I was chicken. And—well, no one wants to be chicken."

Chip's blood boiled. "Chicken!" he repeated angrily. "What's chicken got to do with stealing a truck?" He paused and continued contemptuously, "That's a good one! You let someone talk you into stealing a truck to prove you're not chicken! You must have been out of your mind!"

Chip rose from the desk and began pacing back and forth. Then he paused in front of Eddie and let him have it. "You proved to be just what Tony and Bucky called you, Eddie. Chicken! Chicken because you didn't have enough guts to say, 'No! Not me! I'm not going to get into trouble. Why should I steal a truck?'

"You proved you were chicken all right. Didn't you?" he demanded, pushing Eddie down into the chair beside the desk. "You knuckled down to Tony and Bucky and that very fact proves you went chicken."

Eddie nodded his head in agreement. "Yes, Chip, I guess it does. I never thought about it that way. But, Chip! I know this sounds like an alibi, but I knew you wanted Tony to go to the game and when I tried to give him the tickets he said that I had let him down ever since he got me the job at State Drug and--"

"*He* got you the job?" Chip interrupted. "That's a good one!"

Eddie shook his head and it was obvious that he was trying to choose the right words. "You don't understand, Chip. Tony was the Number One boss and Bucky was the Number Two boss. Tony always decided who got the jobs—the newspaper routes and other kinds of jobs—and he appointed me for the job with you in the drugstore."

"All right, so Tony and Bucky let you get the job. That isn't important. Besides, I had that figured out a long time ago. Now where do these new fellows fit into the picture? The fellows they call Rip and Skids?"

Eddie lowered his eyes and Chip pressed the advantage. "They're running the corner now, aren't they? Haven't they taken over from Tony and Bucky?"

Eddie nodded. "Yes," he managed, in a low voice. Then, gathering confidence, he continued, "Yes, Chip, they have— Why shouldn't they? They're even older than you are! Just as big, too!"

"Taking the truck was their idea, too, wasn't it?"

Eddie was silent for a moment and then the words came with a rush. He told about the arrival of two new families in the neighborhood and the appearance of Rip and Skids on the corner the same evening. "They moved right across the street from us, Chip. And they're always loafing on the front steps or down at the corner. And they've got Tony and Bucky right where they want them. Bucky more than Tony, though."

"What about the truck? What did they want you to do with the truck?"

"I wasn't supposed to do anything with the truck, Chip. Rip and Skids said it was a test for Tony and Bucky. Anyway that's what Tony told me."

"What kind of test?"

"I don't know."

"But where were they taking the truck?"

"Tony never told me exactly, Chip. He said something about leaving the truck in an alley off of Ninth Street and that Rip and Skids would do the rest."

"Were they going to bring it back?"

"I don't know, Chip."

"I still don't understand why *you* had to go."

"I told you, Chip. Tony and Bucky followed me and caught up with me after I left the store and Tony said he wanted me to come because I had to prove my loyalty to him just like he and Bucky had to prove their loyalty to Rip and Skids."

Chip shook his head. "That's a fine definition of loyalty," he said disgustedly. "How in the world could Rip and Skids take the leadership away from Tony and Bucky so quickly and dominate them so easily?"

"Like I said before, Chip, they're *old!* Besides, Rip is a prize fighter, or used to be, and Skids is nearly as tough. And they don't fool around. You tell them you won't do something and you get beat up! Period! They're not afraid of men, either. They've already beat up a couple. For no reason at all, as far as I could see."

That was too much for Chip. He was bewildered. "But didn't the men report them to the police? Why didn't someone tell Pop King? Wouldn't he do something about it if he knew they were beating up everyone in sight?"

"Sure," Eddie said significantly. "If he *knew* it he might. But who's gonna tell him? Not *me!*"

Chip conceded that point and was about to resume his pacing when Soapy interrupted, barging unceremoniously through the door. "C'mon, you guys," he urged. "We gotta get over to the Y for the judo match." He appraised Eddie. "How you feelin', Champ? In the pink?"

"He's all right," Chip said shortly. "You two go ahead. I've got to see Coach Ralston. Good luck, Eddie. I hope you win."

Soapy's cheerful expression vanished. "Aw, no, Chip," he pleaded. "*Aw,* no!"

But Soapy was talking to himself. Chip was gone, threading his way up Main Street through the frenzied football crowd, before Soapy could say "curfew."

CHAPTER 15

TEEN-WEIGHT JUDO CHAMP

CURLY RALSTON was bent over his desk, deeply absorbed in a last-minute review of the Dukes scouting notes. Chip paused at the door and waited, but Ralston was so deep in thought that it was several seconds before the big man sensed that someone was present. Then he saw Chip and he whipped his feet off the desk and swung upright like the recoil of a steel spring. "Hello, Hilton," he said warmly, "you're early."

"I don't think so, sir. I guess that I'm just the opposite. At least I was last night."

"What do you mean?"

"I broke the curfew rule, sir. I was out after eleven o'clock."

Ralston stared at Chip unbelievingly. "I don't understand," he said slowly. "Say that again."

Chip explained that he had gone on a personal errand after work and had been unable to get back to Jeff until nearly midnight. "I'm sorry, Coach," he said simply.

Ralston was caught by surprise. He chewed his underlip and regarded Chip speculatively. It was apparent that he was trying to determine a course of action. He leaned back in his chair and laced his hands behind his head. "I thought George Grayson let his football players off early."

"He does, sir."

"Wasn't it possible for you to take care of this business at some other time?"

"No, sir."

"I see." Ralston studied Chip briefly and then continued, "Is that all? Don't you have anything to add to what you've told me?"

"No, sir," Chip said, "except that it was something personal and that I'm sorry."

Ralston nodded. "I believe that," he said. "All right, Hilton, I'll think it over. Thanks for telling me yourself before someone beat you to it."

Chip paused at the door. "Shall I suit up, sir?"

Ralston deliberated a long second. "Yes," he said, at last, "you can suit up."

Chip retraced his steps and was back at State Drug at eleven-thirty. It had been a short talk and a fast trip but a lot of ground had been covered. And he'd done the right thing; he hadn't been chicken.

Soapy and Eddie returned from the Y shortly after twelve o'clock, the irrepressible redhead broadcasting to anybody who would listen that he was in distinguished company. "This, ladies and gentlemen," he cried, waving a hand grandiloquently toward Eddie Redding, "is the unchallenged *teen-weight* judo champion of University, the state, undoubtedly in the country and, possibly, in the universe."

Eddie was as proud as the heavyweight champion of the world. "I did it, Chip," he cried, "I did it! I beat him two straight falls!"

Soapy's exuberance evaporated as soon as he caught a glimpse of Chip's face. "Bad news?" he asked fearfully.

"I don't know," Chip said. "Come on, let's go."

Outside, Fireball and Whitty and Biggie Cohen had commandeered a taxi which was surrounded by an admiring group. The fans opened up a path and shouted their encouragement as Chip and Soapy piled it. "Go get 'em, Hilton!" "Let's go, Smith!" "State of the Nation, you guys!" "How ya feelin', Biggie?" "Pull in those passes, Whittemore." "Bust that line, Finley!" "Meet all you guys here after the game. Right here! We got to celebrate this one real good!"

In the dressing room, Soapy edged over beside Chip. "What did Ralston say?"

"Nothing. I told him I had broken the curfew rule and asked him if I should suit up and he said yes."

"Did you tell him about me?"

"No, Soapy, I didn't. You—"

Before Chip could finish the sentence, Soapy was on his way, striding purposefully out of the room. A few minutes later he was back, his lips set in a thin, tight line, the freckles standing out brown and clear through the unusual paleness of his complexion. "That's that!" he whispered grimly.

Nothing happened then or in the warm-up drills in the stadium. But when they left the field and gathered in the dressing room for Ralston's last-minute instructions, the entire squad got a shock.

"You'll be playing this game without the services of two of your teammates," Ralston said sharply. "Chip Hilton and Soapy Smith have been benched for failure to observe the eleven-o'clock curfew."

A dead, uncomfortable silence followed Ralston's

words. And that silence seemed to drain all the fight and hustle out of the State team right there in the dressing room. Ralston sensed what had happened to his team as soon as he finished the sentence, but it was done and he was wise enough to realize that further digression would not help the situation.

Nothing else helped that afternoon—helped State's football fortunes, that is. The players were sluggish on the defense, and Ralston's complicated offense fell flat without the wizardry of Chip's ball handling. Burk did his best but the spark just wasn't there. Fortunately, the Dukes had a bad afternoon, too, fumbling just when their ground attack was eating up the first downs and a score seemed imminent, or running into a State interception the few times they ventured into the air. What had promised to be a brilliant battle between two football powers degenerated into a sluggish, uninteresting match.

Watching the Dukes' powerful running attack, Chip remembered Sullivan's scouting analysis. The Dukes followed the coach's description to the letter. They concentrated on basic football, staying with a bone-crushing, head-on personal-contact contest on the ground, and they made you play their game.

Chip had been so wrapped up in his own misery that he had forgotten to look for Eddie and Mark until the end of the first quarter. When he turned to look, Mark saw him and waved and yelled. Chip returned the greeting and was surprised to see Tony Carlara sitting between Eddie and Mark.

And right then, right when the crowd noise stilled, a fan with a fog horn voice began to advise Ralston how to run the team.

"What you savin' Hilton for, Coach, the junior prom?"

"C'mon, Ralston! Put Number 44 in the game!"

Other fans in the vicinity of the side-line coach chimed in and soon it was a chant confied to the fans behind the State bench. But when time was in and the teams were ready to play, the chant had spread and gathered momentum until it was a roar.

"We want Hilton! We want Hilton! We want Hilton!"

The action on the field caught their attention then, and the chant gradually died away. But it came right back when Burk tried a pass which resulted in an interception. And it held straight through to the end of the scoreless half when the teams left the field.

Chip trailed along the side-line with the bench warmers, a blanket covering the big 44 on his back. He was trying to be as inconspicuous as possible. But the fans knew him and recognized him and they hurled questions at him all the way to the runway leading under the stadium.

Ralston caught it, too. But if he heard the caustic criticisms, one would never have guessed it by his bearing. He walked composedly and confidently along beside Rockwell, discussing the play of the first half as unconcernedly as if he were in his own living room.

Chip had never felt so uncomfortable in his life. Nothing was said by any of his teammates, but a wall of restraint was present. He sat down on the hard bench in the dressing room under the stadium, thankful for Mike Murphy's no-talking rule. After the players had been sponged and taped and checked by Mike Murphy and his assistants, Ralston reviewed the first half. He quickly referred to the mistakes, mapped the second-half strategy, and finished by expressing his confidence in their ability to "keep fighting." That was it, and when the second-half starters raced out on the field, Burk was still in at quarterback.

Walking back along the side-line to the bench with Soapy, Chip again waved to Mark and Eddie and checked the occupants of his other seats. He recognized none of the corner crowd he knew, with the exception of Bucky Husta, who was sitting between two older fellows whom he judged to be Rip and Skids. All three were watching him intently.

Chip caught the eye of the fellow on Husta's left. The flashily dressed fellow gestured toward him and shouted mockingly, "Where's the social worker, Coach? Put in the hero! Put in Hilton!"

Soapy heard the raucous voice and pulled back as if he was caught from behind. "Why, you—" he began.

Chip pulled Soapy forward. "Never mind," he said. "Don't pay any attention to him."

Soapy was still glaring angrily at the stranger. "Who's the wise guy?" he asked fiercely. "Why, he's in one of your seats!"

"It's not too important," Chip said.

"That's gratitude!" Soapy raged. "You give 'em free tickets, and they make wisecracks behind your back."

"It's not important," Chip repeated. "Forget *them!* You see where Tony is sitting? That's what I'm interested in."

During the half-time intermission, the rival bands had entertained the fans with formations and music.

But most of the State fans spent the interim trying to find out what was wrong with Chip Hilton.

The newsmen and the broadcasters were as much in the dark as the fans. They had quizzed the State spotters unsuccessfully and were left to vague speculations when the reporter who had volunteered to approach Ralston was politely escorted from the side-lines.

Gee-Gee Gray had been a Hilton booster from the very first day he had seen him in action as a freshman. Now, up in the broadcasting booth, he was beside himself trying to explain why Chip was out of action. "We still don't know what's wrong with Hilton, fans. *If* anything—

"Could be this is one of Curly Ralston's tricks. Could be he's holding his All-America candidate until State is in a scoring position. Now I'm second-guessing one of the greatest coaches in the business. Hmmmm.

"Well, since I've taken over the State coaching job, I might as well go whole hog and try third-guessing. Hilton's a pretty valuable piece of football material, right? Now, suppose Ralston got to figuring the Dukes are rough on passers, and since the game has no bearing on the conference championship, he might be holding Hilton out to avoid an injury! You don't go for that! Hmmm.

"Guess I don't care for that, either! Not like Ralston! Not like Hilton! The kid can take care of himself in any company.

"Now this is the last try. Honest! Hilton could have a Charley horse or a sprained ankle. Could be.

"The teams are back on the field now, and State will kick off. Ralston's starting his seven blocks of granite on the line—the Suicide Seven! Whittemore and Higgins at the ends! Cohen and Maxim, tackles! Two seniors in the guard spots, McCarthy and Clark. And the old reliable, Captain Mike Brennan at center.

"In the backfield, Ralston is starting the same foursome which he sent out on the field for the first half: Morris, Finley, Gibbons, and Burk. Ace Gibbons will kick for State. There's no score here in the stadium at University in the game between State and the Dukes.

"Gibbons boots a high one! It's down to Jones on the Dukes' twenty-yard stripe. He's up to the twenty-five, the thirty, and he's downed by Tiny Tim McCarthy on the—let's say—the thirty-two-yard line.

"Here comes a naked reverse by Kytes and he's really moving—but he'll go nowhere. Biggie Cohen has him cornered—Oh! What a tackle! Wait a minute, there's a flag on the play.

"It's a penalty against State. It's an automatic first and ten at the spot of the foul. That places the ball on the Dukes' forty-six.

"Reed carries. First down! Reed got eleven yards on the play. That moves the ball down to the State forty-three-yard line. It will be first and ten! Kytes is at right half, Reed at quarterback, Jones at fullback, and Wheat at left halfback.

"Jones has the ball. He's racing through left tackle. Oops, there's a flag on the play. Dukes' backfield in motion. Captain Mike Brennan accepts the penalty, so it's first and fifteen for the Dukes on the State forty-eight. Brennan would probably have declined the penalty so the down would count, but Jones had carried the ball clear down to the State thirty-five-yard line . . ."

Gee-Gee Gray's broadcast the rest of the afternoon was strictly reportorial, an unvarnished word picture of an uninteresting game which ended in a scoreless tie. Gray did say just before the game went off the air that Curly Ralston was to be his guest on his seven-o'clock sports roundup and that he was sure the Chip Hilton story would be clarified at that time.

There was no snake dance and very little celebrating after the game, although the fans could very well have accorded State that honor. Holding the mighty Dukes to a tie was no mean accomplishment.

Chip was tired and stiff from sitting the bench. And sitting is right, for there had been no action in the game exciting enough to bring him to his feet. He looked for Eddie and Mark and Tony when the game ended, but they were gone, lost in the crowd of fans filing out of the stands. Before he could move, it seemed, he was surrounded by reporters.

"What happened, Hilton? You hurt?"

"How come you didn't play?"

"What's the matter with *you,* Smith?"

A photographer came pushing through, adjusting his camera. "Hold it, fellows. I've got to have a picture."

Soapy moved back for the picture, but Chip stopped him. "I think you'd better ask the coach," he said. "Come on, Soapy. We've got to go to work."

The excuse worked with the photographer, but not with the sports writers. They pressed around Chip and Soapy in a solid ring, backed up now by side-line pass officials and fans who had reached the field. "Why didn't you play?" they demanded. "How come you sat the bench?"

Chip had never been in such a spot. He didn't know what to do or say, and, after the photographer incident, Soapy wasn't talking to anyone. Henry Rockwell saved the day. Rock did not know why Chip had broken curfew but he knew there had to be a good reason behind the infraction. He saw the milling group, nudged Ralston, and led the way through the crowd until he and the head coach were by Chip's side.

"The coach will answer the questions, fellows," Rockwell said, addressing the newsmen. He grasped Chip and Soapy each by an arm and gently started them toward the end of the field. "You two hit the showers."

Chip and Soapy trotted gratefully away, and Ralston answered the questions, advising the reporters that Hilton and Smith had been benched for breaking the eleven-o'clock curfew and that more drastic action other than today's benching would have been their lot except for the fact that they worked every night until 10:45 P.M.

"That doesn't give them much of a margin to get back to their quarters by eleven o'clock," Ralston explained, "and that's why they were not suspended from the squad. They are reinstated as of now," he continued, "and I expect to use them in the Midwestern game next Saturday. I might add, gentlemen, that Hilton and Smith reported the matter themselves."

"And you want to be a sports reporter!" Soapy said scornfully, as he and Chip made their way through the runway. "Why, they'd tear a fellow to pieces to get a story!"

"They sure would," Chip agreed dourly.

Chip's teammates were in various stages of undress when he and Soapy entered the dressing room. There was no conversation except for a mur-

mur of disgust and self-condemnation from the subdued players. Biggie and Whitty and Speed and Fireball and Red Schwartz immediately surrounded them, while other members of the squad merely looked up and as quickly looked away. Captain Mike Brennan was the exception, joining Chip's pals.

"What happened, Chip?" Brennan asked. "Tough break. We needed you out there this afternoon. Needed you and Smith both."

"We just couldn't make it home before eleven o'clock last night," Chip said. "We're sorry, Mike. We're sorry we let you and the team down."

"Who reported you?" Ace Gibbons demanded, joining Brennan. "It was a dirty trick!"

"No one reported us, Ace," Chip said quietly. "We told the coach ourselves."

Tiny Tim McCarthy closed his locker with a bang. "You'd think he'd have given you a break," he growled, "knowing you work every night! I don't see how you do it. Classes and studying and football and working! It's not—"

Tiny Tim cut off the words as if he had bitten his tongue, and gestured toward the door. Curly Ralston and Henry Rockwell were standing there, waiting quietly. The two coaches hesitated a second, and then advanced to the center of the dressing room.

"That's all right, Tim," Ralston said gently. "I heard what you were saying and I agree to a point. However, Hilton and Smith *did* break the rule and that left me no alternative." He paused and looked at Chip and Soapy. "Particularly," he added significantly, "when they would give no explanation!"

CHAPTER 16

YOU CAN'T WIN 'EM ALL

STATE's football fans had expected to win the game with the Dukes—secretly, that is, they expected to do so—and their confidence had been rudely shaken. But their loyalty was sure and strong, and the general philosophy heard all over University was expressed by Tims Lansing that evening when he dropped in to see Chip. "Hiya, Chip," he said cheerily, "you can't win 'em all!"

"I wish the fellows could have won this one," Chip said. "Especially since—"

"I know," Lansing interrupted. "I heard the coach on Gray's sports broadcast. He's a great guy. He said the fellows put up a great fight—said he was proud of their showing.

"Say, I've been thinking about the field-goal reputation you've acquired. You know, every team you play realizes you're Mister Toe in person whenever State gets inside their forty-yard line.

"Now, why wouldn't it be a good idea to work up a fake-kick play when you need six or seven points instead of three?"

"Sounds good," Chip agreed.

Lansing eyed Chip keenly as he pulled a piece of

paper out of his inside pocket. "Thought you would say that, so I worked up a little play on my own. It's a perfect take-off for the place-kick formation the coach has been using." He spread the paper on the desk. "What do you think of it?"

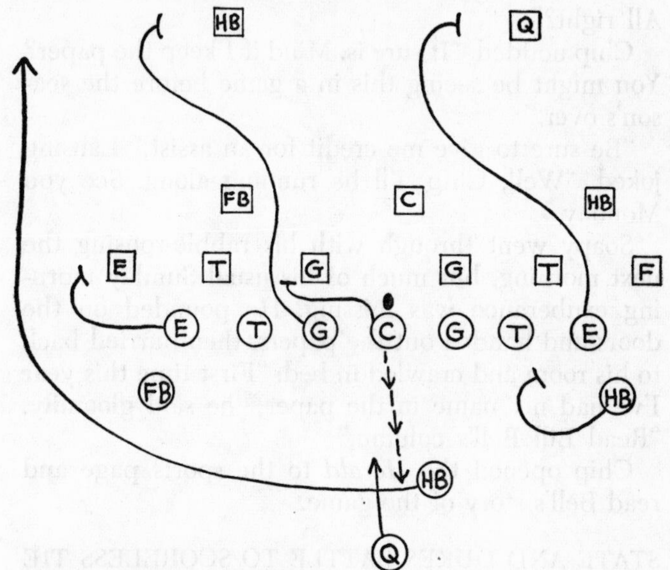

Chip scanned the outline. "It looks fine," he said. "I like it."

Lansing beamed. "It *is* good. You know why? Because Morris is fast and runs well to the left. Another thing. Every team in the conference lines up in a 6–3–2 defense formation when they expect a place kick. And all of them play their line backers up close, and that makes the blocking easier for a wide end sweep. Right?"

"Right!" Chip echoed.

Lansing grinned with satisfaction and continued. "The pass is to Morris naturally, and you do just as always—take your step and kick. Only the ball isn't there. Morris has it and he's running around left end. Morris has to be sure to have his knee off the ground when he catches the ball, and when you kick through his arms he's got to hold the ball in his left hand. All right?"

Chip nodded. "It sure is. Mind if I keep the paper? You might be seeing this in a game before the season's over."

"Be sure to give me credit for an assist," Lansing joked. "Well, Chip, I'll be running along. See you Monday."

Soapy went through with his rabble-rousing the next morning, but much of his usual Sunday morning exuberance was missing. He pounded on the doors and handed out the papers, then hurried back to his room and crawled in bed. "First time this year I've had my name in the paper," he said gloomily. "Read Bill Bell's column."

Chip opened the *Herald* to the sports page and read Bell's story of the game.

STATE AND DUKES BATTLE TO SCORELESS TIE

State Misses Star Field General

By Bill Bell

State and the Dukes concentrated on old-fashioned football this afternoon and proved the old saw of the irresistible force and the immovable object. The sixty minutes of straight football was not appealing to the 48,756 fans and students who packed the stadium, but it was an exhibition of line play at its best.

Both forward walls were superb in their offensive and defensive play.

State played without the services of Chip Hilton, sensational sophomore quarterback, who was benched by Coach Curly Ralston for a violation of training rules. A teammate, Soapy Smith, was benched for the same reason. . . .

"It's not as bad as I thought it would be," Chip said.

Soapy grunted. "Read Locke's story in the *News*," he said shortly, waiting for Chip's reaction.

Chip found Locke's story without much difficulty. In fact, it practically jumped out of the sports page at him.

STATE AND DUKES TIE
HILTON BENCHED, TEAM DEMORALIZED
Fumbles Disastrous to Dukes
BY JIM LOCKE

The Dukes were in a gratuitous mood yesterday afternoon in the State stadium. They fumbled conveniently and often, and if the locals had been playing any kind of football, their record this morning would not be marred with a tie.

Coach Curly Ralston benched quarterback Chip Hilton for a training violation just prior to the game, and this abrupt decision completely demoralized the State squad. Hilton would make no statement, but Ralston advised the press that the star quarterback had been penalized for breaking a curfew regulation.

Thousands of State fans and this writer are wondering just whom Ralston punished by benching Hilton. It would seem that the penalty was directed more toward State than toward Hilton. Ralston's poor timing undoubtedly upset his team and rendered them incapable of taking advantage of the multitudinous number of breaks which were offered them all afternoon.

Although the game had no bearing on the conference standings, it further solidified this writer's opinion that Ralston's sophomore team is beginning to come apart at the seams, and that further day dreams or nightmares about winning the conference championship had better be discarded.

"Well?" Soapy demanded, as Chip dropped the paper.

Chip shook his head and pressed his lips together in a grim line. "That's not fair to the coach. Why, Locke practically blames him for not winning the game. Why didn't he criticize me? It was my fault. Guess I'll go downstairs and study. Coming?"

"You crazy? Not me! This is my day for hibernating!"

After church and lunch, Chip took a long nap and then spent the rest of the afternoon and evening in study. His pals tried to coax him out for a walk but Chip had his work organized and stuck with it until ten o'clock. Then he went to bed, his heart still heavy with thoughts of the game.

Ralston and his assistants "poured it on" Monday afternoon. The tie with the Dukes had no bearing on the conference standing but it had been a shock. Now they were determined there would be no let down in preparing for tough Midwestern, unpredictable Wesleyan, and mighty A. & M. There was no bitterness or disappointment apparent in the bearing of the members of the coaching staff but each one, from Ralston down, was dead serious about his work. Chip was dead serious, too. He couldn't help feeling self-conscious about being benched, although none of his teammates indicated in any way that they held him responsible for the tie game.

That evening, Herb Miller, the physical director at the Y, dropped by and asked him if he would appear on a boxing show that had been scheduled for Thursday night. "Eddie here is on the program," he said, shaking hands with Chip's assistant, "and it's the big event of the year. If we could advertise that you would take part, it would go over with a bang! Eddie tells me you're pretty nifty with your dukes, and if you and I could put on a three-round exhibition it would bring down the house. What do you say? There won't be anything to it as far as the boxing is concerned. It will be more fun than anything else."

"I haven't boxed since I was in high school," Chip protested. "You'd kill me! Besides, I don't think Coach Ralston would like it."

"He said it would be all right," Miller said quickly. "He just wanted to be sure you would wear a boxing helmet and that we would use twelve-ounce gloves. Gosh, I haven't boxed three rounds since I was in college. One thing is for sure, you're in better condition than I am. If I had to run the length of a football field just once, I'd keel over. Oh, yes, I spoke to Mr. Grayson and he was tickled pink. He's on the Y board, you know."

Chip mentally kicked himself for having told Eddie that he could box, and, against his better judgment, permitted Miller to persuade him to appear on the program. A second later he was sorry. But Eddie was a wide-eyed witness and Chip couldn't back down. "I'll be there," he said reluctantly.

Chip was there Thursday night all right, and so was Frank Caruso and another man about his age and size, and Eddie and Mark and Tony and Bucky and practically every kid from the Tenth Street corner. And they nearly raised the roof when Eddie Redding entered the ring for his judo demonstration. Chip sat in the rear of the crowd talking with the Y secretary. He was amazed at the progress Eddie had made in the short space of time he had concentrated on the sport. Then Herb Miller came back and said it was time for them to get dressed.

Chip was recognized when he walked up through the crowd. The youngsters rose and applauded him all the way down the aisle. And when he climbed through the ropes and was introduced by the Y secretary, they nearly tore down the place, stamping their feet and applauding until the man raised his hands for quiet. There wasn't much question about their admiration for State's varsity quarterback.

It really wasn't much of a boxing exhibition. Chip was in far better condition than Miller, and at the end of the third round had the instructor out on his feet. Miller grinned admiringly when it was over and threw one arm over his rival's shoulder and raised Chip's other arm and hand in the air. "The winner, gentlemen," he cried, "and still champion!"

Frank Caruso and his friend and Mark and Eddie were waiting for him in the lobby. The candy-store proprietor introduced Tony's father. "This is Tony's old man," he said. "Mr. Chip meet Mr. Tony Carlara, Senior."

Mr. Carlara greeted Chip warmly, gripping his hand and smiling. "I'm very glad to meet you, Mr. Chip."

"My name is Hilton, Mr. Carlara. I know your son."

The little man smiled. "You know my Tony? That's good. Maybe you come visit my house sometime."

"I'd be glad to come. Well, excuse me, Mr. Carlara, Mr. Caruso. Eddie and I have to hustle back to work. You going with us, Mark?"

Mark nodded and they hurried back to State Drug and back to the stockroom. Soapy was right behind them, bearing two containers of malted milks, words flying. "How'd you make out, Eddie, Chip? Ya beat 'em, huh? Atta boy! I knew you would! Drink this, Champ! What *you* doin' here, Mark? Drink that and get goin'! You got school tomorrow. You too, Eddie."

Mark nodded but he made no effort to leave. He looked from Chip to Eddie and covertly rolled his eyes toward the door. Soapy got it and reacted as if he was pulling out of the line to run interference on an end run. "You want a soda, Chip? I'll send it back with Eddie. C'mon, Eddie."

As soon as the door closed behind them, Chip turned to the big-little Redding. "What's on your mind, Mark?"

"Eddie's in bad with Rip and Skids, Chip. Guess they think he snitched about the truck. Anyway, they said he worked with you and that was the only way you *could* know. They said a lot of other things, Chip. Said you wouldn't get away with it the next time."

"What did they mean?"

"I guess they meant you going down there and catching Tony and Bucky and Eddie. I guess they meant they'd beat you up!"

CHAPTER 17

CRISIS AND SHOWDOWN

George Grayson was a quiet and unobtrusive man, but he was always available when friends needed help. The proprietor of State Drug was a family man with a house full of daughters but he had never been blessed with a son. His friends thought that was the chief reason behind his efforts to help so many young men through school. The friendly man made it possible for his employees to go to college by assigning them special hours through the days and evenings so they could carry a full schedule of classes.

Most of those who were familiar with Grayson's background knew the real reason; knew that he was reliving his own college days, times when he had to struggle through day after day of heartbreaking work and study and privation to secure an education. Narrow-minded and jealous competitors said it was because he wanted to cash in on the business and publicity which fellows like Chip Hilton, Fireball Finley, Philip Whittemore, and Soapy Smith brought to State Drug.

Whatever his reason, there was no doubt about

his enthusiasm for football. Friday evening he personally drove his football employees to the railroad station to meet the Midnight Limited bound for Green Mountain and the all-important conference battle with Midwestern.

The station was a madhouse! The platform was worse. George Grayson and Chip and his pals were caught up in the jam of fans and students who had come to give the team a royal send-off. Everyone was talking at once; none of the managers could be found, and Chip and his crowd did not know the number of their Pullman car or the numbers of their compartments. But it was the right train, and, once they were aboard, it didn't make much difference. They dumped their suitcases in a corner of one of the cars and waited in an empty Pullman seat until the head manager found them and assigned them to their car and compartments.

There was the usual excitement that is present on a game trip, but Chip and Soapy locked the door of their compartment and went to bed. They breakfasted in the dining car at eight o'clock. When the train arrived in Green Mountain at ten o'clock, a bus was waiting to take them to their hotel. Ralston had a team pregame snack ordered for eleven-thirty, and it was time to eat again before they could turn around. At twelve o'clock they were on their way to Midwestern Stadium and by twelve-thirty were suited up.

Midwestern was playing before a "homecoming" crowd, and the players were determined and full of fight. It was a tough game, a battle of two strong defensive teams. Midwestern kicked to Morris and Speed brought the ball back to the thirty-yard line. Chip started at quarterback and tested the home team's pass defense on the first down, hiding the ball with fakes and flipping a quick buttonhook to Larry Higgins which was good for seven yards.

"Zone-pass defense," Chip reported in the huddle. "We'll use Z passes until they change. Now let's try forty-six on a count of three! Hike!"

Fireball drove straight ahead over center and Chip faked to give him the ball; faked again to Speed cutting toward the right flat, pivoted left, and aimed the ball toward Whittemore driving downfield near the left side-line. Then he twisted back and winged a hard pass to Speed far out in the right flat. It was a zone, all right. The wing flanker hit Speed as soon as he caught the ball. Chip noticed that the middle backer trailed along the line of scrimmage.

Chip glanced quickly at the middle zone. The defense had shifted to the right with the middle guard filling the hole. "Good defense," he muttered. "Tough!"

And tough it was! Both teams played a tight defense. Midwestern scored twice in the first half and kicked both extra points. State tallied on a touchdown and Chip kicked the extra point. The score at the end of the half was: Midwestern 14, State 7.

State came back fighting in the second half, holding Midwestern for no gain on the twenty after Chip kicked the ball into the end zone. Midwestern punted and Speed took the hard-drilling spiral on State's forty-five-yard line and carried ten to the home team's forty-five. Then State marched on the ground to the twelve, where the Midwestern line stiffened and held. On third down, ten to go, Chip sent Finley wide around right end. The big fellow was forced toward the side-line and for a moment it looked like he would be thrown for a big loss. At the last instant he fired a desperate pass clear across the field to Speed who was standing all alone in the far corner of the end zone. Speed couldn't miss the catch and Chip didn't miss the extra point. That tied up the score at 14–14.

The two teams battled furiously and evenly in the fourth quarter, the ball changing hands half a dozen times. Chip's long, high punts gradually began to tell, and as the clock ran out, State had the ball on the Midwestern fifteen-yard-line, fourth down and eight to go. Every fan in the stadium knew what was coming and the old familiar "Block that kick! Block that kick! Block that kick!" came sweeping down on the players from all sides. Chip and Speed collaborated perfectly on the kick, and the ball sailed end over end and straight through the middle of the uprights. State had won its sixth straight conference game, 17 to 14.

The train was jammed with fans going back to University, and the aisles became a sort of State campus as enthusiasts and celebrants wandered through the cars. Chip and Soapy and Speed and Biggie and Whitty and Fireball and Red Schwartz had turned back two cross-aisle seats and were discussing Tims Lansing's play. "It will work in the right spot," Fireball said. "It's simple enough."

"Yes, but the other team would have to think we were going to kick the field goal for sure," Speed said. "And that means everyone would have to do a good faking job of blocking out or I'd end up in the bleachers."

"What's this?" a familiar voice boomed. "Someone trying to steal my job?"

Chip knew that voice all right. He had sensed Ralston's presence when his pals quieted so suddenly. He looked up and grinned. "They would have to be awfully good," he said, rising to his feet.

"Sit down, sit down," Ralston said. "Now, what's the play?"

"It's a play Tims Lansing worked up, Coach," Chip explained. "He figured that it might work when the other team was expecting a placement." He handed the piece of paper to Ralston and continued, "It's a whole lot like our K 66, sir, except in that play the kicker actually kicks at the ball. It's up to Speed or whoever is holding the ball to pull it back at the last second." He studied Ralston's reaction. "What do you think, sir?"

"Not bad," Ralston said, studying the paper. "Not bad at all. I think I'd make one or two little changes, though. Make it a little tougher on the kicker. I'd let him run through the ball all right, but then I'd have him chase the middle backer and send the center down for the block on the defensive right halfback. Got a pencil, Rock?" He sketched the play quickly on the back of Chip's paper. "Here, like this!"

Ralston handed the paper back to Chip and waited. "What do you think? Any better?"

Chip nodded. "Much better."

"Keep in mind," Ralston continued, "that the line would have to hold for at least a three-count before sliding left to get good blocking angles. Another thing. Morris has to keep his right hand and arm out straight and let you kick right through it. And he's got to keep the ball hidden with his left hand. Suppose you study it a bit." He glanced around the circle of faces and grinned. "Looks as if you've got about everyone who is in on the play right here. All but Brennan. Right, Rock?"

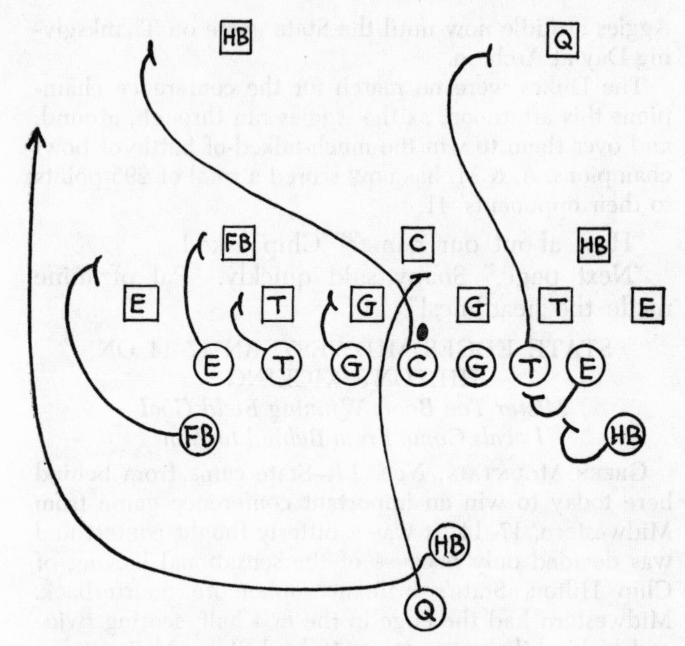

Chip and his pals talked over the play and then hit the sack. The humming of the wheels on the rails was soothing after the hard game, and Chip was soon asleep. It seemed only a few minutes until Soapy shook his shoulder and thrust a Sunday newspaper under his nose. "Something to think about," Soapy said, pointing to the headline.

A. & M. DEFEATS DUKES 21–7 FOR SIXTEENTH STRAIGHT

Iron Men's First Loss in Sixteen Games

ARCHTON, *Nov. 13*—A. & M. won its sixteenth consecutive victory today, downing the invincible Dukes for their first loss in sixteen games. A. & M. has now won nine straight this season, extending the Aggie consecutive victory string to sixteen straight over a two-year period. The

Aggies are idle now until the State game on Thanksgiving Day at Archton.

The Dukes were no match for the conference champions this afternoon, as the Aggies ran through, around, and over them to win the much-talked-of battle of bowl champions. A. & M. has now scored a total of 295 points to their opponents' 41.

"How about our game?" Chip asked.

"Next page," Soapy said quickly. "Pal of mine made the headlines!"

STATE EDGES MIDWESTERN 17–14 ON HILTON'S KICKING

Mister Toe Boots Winning Field Goal
Locals Come From Behind to Win

GREEN MOUNTAIN, *Nov. 13*—State came from behind here today to win an important conference game from Midwestern, 17–14. It was a bitterly fought contest and was decided only because of the sensational kicking of Chip Hilton, State's brilliant sophomore quarterback. Midwestern had the edge in the first half, scoring twice and kicking the extra points to lead State, 14–7.

But Chip Hilton, playing his first game in two weeks, proved that he is one of the finest quarterbacks in the country. He piloted his team brilliantly to a 14–14 tie and then used his superior punting ability to pin Midwestern back in its own territory most of the final period. The margin of victory was a three-point field goal from the Midwestern 15-yard line by Hilton as the game ended.

State unquestionably looms as a serious contender for conference honors, despite the brilliant record of A. & M. Wesleyan is the sole remaining obstacle which State must hurdle to qualify as a challenger to A. & M. leadership.

On the basis of comparative scores, State should not have too much difficulty with the Ministers.

"One to go," Soapy observed, when Chip finished the story. "We'll kill 'em!"

The platform was jammed again at University when the Limited pulled in at ten o'clock. Chip and Soapy took a taxi to Jeff and then went to church. After the services, Soapy headed back to Jeff for his Sunday afternoon snooze and Chip started down to Pete's restaurant for lunch. Just as he turned the corner of Main and Tenth, he met Eddie's aunt. They chatted a few minutes about football and then talked about Eddie and the neighborhood problems.

"Eddie is a good boy, Chip. Frail and weak physically—although I must say that you're doing wonders with him—but he has a fine mind and a wonderful attitude. Sometimes he acts more like the head of the family than his father. But he needs help. In fact, all the children in the neighborhood need help. They need leadership. Leadership by someone the boys respect and admire, someone with ideals and ambitions.

"If my brother John would only assume the responsibilities of the boys, things would be different. I can handle the girls, but the boys need a man to help them. But John gets discouraged and locks himself in his room and stays there. But here I am talking all about myself and my troubles when it's such a nice day and a young man like you should be enjoying himself. I hope you'll come to see us soon. Good-by."

The State campus was buzzing conference championship the next week. Chip had become a campus hero and he didn't like it. Perhaps that's a little too strong. He liked it but he wished his fellow students would be a little more conservative in discussing his feats. Everything seemed to be going too smoothly and he had a feeling it was too good to last. Eddie was his old self, smiling and cheerful. "Tony is my best friend now," he advised Chip one evening. "You going to have the tickets this week?"

"I'll have the tickets all right," Chip assured him. "Ten of them!"

Later that evening, Mark came in for his nightly malted and ice cream and told Chip that Tony was a different sort of a person. "He's been coming up to the house with Eddie almost every night," he confided. "He and Rip had some kind of an argument. Anyway, Tony doesn't hang around the corner any more."

"How about Bucky?"

"Oh, he hangs around down on the corner with Rip and Skids all the time."

"Don't Rip and Skids work?"

"Gee, no, Chip. I heard them talking to the guys on the corner one night and Rip was saying that only stupid guys work."

"Where do they get their clothes and spending money? They always seem to be dressed up."

Mark snorted. "Dressed up! Huh! You call those long coats and tight trousers dressed up? Huh, I wouldn't be seen dead in clothes like that! Makes me sick!" Mark ate his last spoonful of ice cream and smacked his lips. "Well," he said, "guess I'd better go home."

Chip visited with Frank Caruso several times that week and learned that Frank and Tony's father, and some of the other men in the neighborhood, were organizing so they could do something about the kids. At Chip's suggestion, Caruso promised to ask Mr. Redding to join forces with them.

The Thanksgiving vacation began on Friday. Chip met Pop King in Pete's restaurant and joined him in a cup of coffee. During the course of the conversation he asked Pop if he knew Rip and Skids.

"Sure I know 'em, Chip. Been watching them grow up over on the North Side. Nineteenth Street. Just moved down here in this neighborhood. I'm watching 'em. They've been picked up a couple of times but nothing serious. Rip used to be a club fighter of sorts. He's a tough youngster. Guess I shouldn't call him a youngster any more, though. Must be twenty-two or thereabouts."

"Isn't there any way you can keep them away from the kids?"

"No. About all I can do is to tell 'em to move on. But they come right back."

"What's their last names?"

"Grasco and Welks. Rip Grasco and Skids Welks. I don't know exactly why they're hanging around the kids on the corner, but I'll bet my badge it's for no good!"

That night, trouble was back. Eddie was wearing his whipped dog expression and had gone back in his shell. Mark came in later and Chip sent Eddie out with some syrups for the fountain.

"What's wrong with Eddie, Mark?"

"He was crying last night after we went to bed, Chip. Rip and Skids and Bucky slapped him around."

"What for?"

"They caught him coming home from work. I guess it was something about him and Tony and not reporting or something like that."

"Reporting?"

"Well, it's the same with Tony. He stopped hanging around the corner and they had a showdown with him and said they'd make him a lieutenant or something. Looks like they got Tony scared, although he stood right up to them. Anyway, Eddie wouldn't join or report whatever they call it, and they beat him up.

"They boss the whole neighborhood now. They're nothing but bullies but I'm getting tougher. Feel my arm!"

Eddie came back then and quietly did his work. But Chip noticed that he looked at Mark warningly. A few minutes later Mark said good night and left for home. When it was time for Eddie to leave, Chip gave him the tickets for the game and was surprised by the boy's sudden reluctance to accept them.

"What's the matter, Eddie? Are you in trouble again?"

"No, Chip, I'm fine. I'm just tired, I guess."

"You look tired. You go on home and get a good night's rest."

Eddie's attitude disturbed Chip and after the youngster left he made a hasty decision. He closed and locked the stockroom door and told Mitzi he would be back in twenty minutes. Then he hurried out the Tenth Street door. He looked down Tenth Street but Eddie was not in sight. In fact, there wasn't a soul walking down Tenth. Chip glanced quickly toward Main and caught sight of Eddie just as he turned the corner. Chip trailed him and kept the boy in sight all the way down Main Street.

The neighborhood gradually changed, from stores to dwellings, and then to the slum area. Up ahead, Eddie hurried purposefully along, then turned to the right and vanished up an alley. Chip quickened his pace and entered the dark opening. Eddie had stopped at his own street and was carefully peering around the corner.

Chip waited in the darkness. Then Eddie suddenly

streaked around the corner. Chip heard someone yell and he sprinted forward. At the corner he paused and scanned the scene. Eddie was racing for his house in the middle of the block, and tearing down the street from the candy-store corner were three shadowy figures. Then Eddie sprang up the steps and slammed the Redding front door almost in the faces of Bucky and Rip Grasco and Skids Welks.

Chip breathed a sigh of relief and turned back down the alley. Now the picture was clear. The crisis had arrived and the showdown could no longer be postponed.

CHAPTER 18

MAKES A FOOTBALL TALK

CHIP tried to put Eddie's predicament out of mind when he went to bed later that night, but it couldn't be done. He tossed and turned all night and started for State Drug just as the sun peeked over the horizon. By the time Soapy and Fireball and Whitty and Mitzi Savrill and the rest of the staff checked in, Chip's usual Saturday morning work was all finished. He waited impatiently for Eddie to put in an appearance. But nine o'clock passed and then ten, and eleven, and eleven-thirty, and no Eddie—and, no Mark. Then the excitement of the game caught up with him and partly forced him to forget his two little pals.

It was a beautiful football day: cool, crisp, and clear, but with enough haze in the sky to eliminate the glare of the sun. The stands were nearly filled when State lined up to kick off to Wesleyan. And somewhere in the giant bowl, gossip had it, the entire A. & M. squad and coaching staff were on hand to have a look-see at the Statesmen.

Chip looked over behind the bench and was surprised to see that his seats were filled with strangers. All except the three on the end. Bucky and Rip and Skids were seated in these and appeared to be watching him intently. Then the game whistle shrilled and Chip forgot everything except the ball sitting up on the tee, six short strides away.

The game progressed according to form. Wesleyan could not gain and punted to Chip on the forty-yard line, and he carried it back to the Ministers' forty. Then State scored in exactly four plays and Chip kicked the extra point. So, at the end of the first three minutes of play, State led, 7 to 0. Ralston sent in a whole new team in the middle of the first period and that gave Chip a chance to look for Eddie and Mark. But they were not in sight, not in his seats, or anywhere behind them in the section.

Chip got back in the game at the start of the second half, and as he ran out on the field, he heard the raucous voice he had associated with Rip Grasco yell something about "social worker!" His blood boiled and he promised himself a chance to take care of that individual at the first opportunity.

The second half would have been a slaughter had Ralston kept his regulars in the game and given them free rein. But the wily mentor worked his squad under wraps, limiting the attack to straight on-the-ground football, and used his first string sparingly. Chip started the third quarter but Ralston pulled him right after the kickoff. He got his last chance in the final four-minute period when Ralston sent him in to boot a field goal from the Wesleyan twenty-five-yard line. The kick was good and ended the scoring for both sides. The final score was: State 40, Wesleyan 14.

As soon as the game ended, Chip sprinted off the

field and over to the section behind the State bench. Rip and Skids and Bucky were walking slowly away. Chip grabbed Bucky by the arm and swung him around. "Where's Eddie?" he demanded.

Bucky was surprised and cowed for an instant. "How do I know?" he snarled, jerking away.

"Yeah, and what do we care?" Rip Grasco added nastily. He nudged Skids Welks as Chip faced him. "Looks tough with all that padding on, doesn't he, Skids?"

"Yeah," Skids agreed, "ain't that a laugh!"

Chip ignored them and turned back to Bucky. "Where'd you get the ticket for that seat?" he demanded.

"None of your business," Bucky said boldly. "I got it, didn't I?"

"Yeah," Rip added, "he got it the same place I got mine. Want to make something out of it?"

Chip eyed Rip steadily, nodding his head. "Yes," he said calmly, "I do. It wouldn't be a bad idea at all. I'll see *you* later."

"Any time, social worker," Rip sneered. "Any time, anywhere!"

"Remember just that," Chip said. "Any time, anywhere." He turned away and trotted for the runway. Now to find out what had happened to Eddie and Mark.

The State dressing room was in an uproar. But above the bedlam Chip could hear Soapy yelling, "Move over, Notre Dame, you got company!"

Ralston and Rockwell were watching the celebration. Finally Murph Kelly got the team quieted down long enough for the head coach to make an announcement. Ralston was grinning from ear to ear and Chip got the impression that it wouldn't take much for the head coach to shed his dignity and join in the fun.

"Nice going, men," he said gleefully. "You've come a long way since October second. Not that I ever doubted that you could do it, once you realized your strength. I want to add the congratulations of the staff to all those you're going to receive tonight and tomorrow—

"Now, I don't want to throw cold water on your happiness, but I want to remind you, as I have so many times this season—" he paused and grinned briefly—"thank goodness, that one victory or seven victories do not make a season. We still have the big one to go—the one for the championship!

"So, there is no curfew tonight. But beginning tomorrow, Sunday, and continuing right through the week until we beat A. & M. on Thanksgiving Day afternoon at Archton, all training regulations including a strict curfew check are in effect.

"Thursday afternoon will come all too soon. We'll be leaving here Wednesday morning on the eleven-forty train and work out that afternoon on the A. & M. freshman field. A. & M.'s athletic department has guaranteed us strict privacy for the practice sessions. That's all."

State Drug was jammed that night with celebrants and customers. The entire crew was kept on the go. Eddie didn't show up and neither did Mark, and Chip was worried. "I'll just go down there and find out what's wrong," he muttered. "Right after work!"

Then, at eight o'clock, Mark walked in, Soapy right behind him. Mark's face was scratched and he had a cut lip and the beginning of a gorgeous black eye.

"What happened to you?" Chip gasped.

Mark ignored the question. "Eddie's sick," he said. "He had some trouble with Bucky." He went on to explain that Eddie had started to work that morning and Bucky was waiting for him. "They had a fight, Chip, and Eddie got Bucky down and had him whipped until Skids pulled him off. Then Tony came running out of the house and jumped on Skids, and Rip took on Eddie, and I just hit everybody.

"Then Rip and Skids took the football tickets away from Eddie. It's been some day! Say, I heard ya won!"

"Why didn't you call me or come in earlier? I've been worried."

"Well, Pop's got a job at last. He works from four o'clock to midnight, and Aunt Edith wouldn't let me out of the house until she had to go shopping. So after she put the girls to sleep and told Eddie to watch them, she took me with her to get the groceries. She's smart! She goes down to the river markets after they close on Saturday nights and that way she gets a lot of things cheap. Sometimes she gets things for nothing. I always help her carry them home," he said proudly.

"Who gave you the black eye?" Soapy asked.

"Gee, I don't know. Guess I've got to study some more judo. I didn't do so good."

"I guess not," Chip said dryly.

"The jerks!" Soapy exploded. "How long we gonna let them get away with this?"

"Never mind," Chip said, motioning toward the door, "you go back to work. I want to talk to Mark privately."

After Soapy left, Mark said, "They've got some kind of a meeting Tuesday night, Chip, and Eddie's scared. Rip and Skids said they had to go away for a couple of days, but when they got back he was going to be disciplined. Pop will be at work and I don't know what to do."

"Let me figure it out, Mark. What time are they going to have this meeting?"

"I guess it will be at night down in the alley. They always meet on the corner and then go down in the alley where Mr. Caruso keeps his truck. That's where they hang out when they're playing games or cookin' up something."

"Isn't it pretty dark in the alley?"

"Oh, you can see all right. But they always hold court and settle the arguments there. Most of the time at night, so they can get away if Pop King tries to bust it up."

"I see," Chip said thoughtfully. "Now, Mark, I'll be studying at home all day and working every evening. If Eddie meets Rip or Skids or goes down to that alley any time, day or night, you call me. Understand? No matter what time it is, call me. Here's the number at Jeff. Now don't lose it and don't forget."

Mark straightened his square little shoulders. "I won't," he promised. "And, Chip, you won't tell Eddie I snitched—I mean, you won't tell him I was here, will you?"

Chip shook his head. "No, I won't tell him. I won't tell him anything. Now you run along and meet your aunt."

The next morning, Soapy was back on the job as Jeff's Sunday newspaper distributor. "C'mon, Chipper," he said cheerily, tramping about the room, "read all about it! Read all about the championship bout scheduled for Thanksgiving Day when the Indefatigable Invincibles, meaning State of course, and the Farinaceous Farriers, long for Aggies, meet for the championship of all points north, south, east, and west, including the upside-down bowl! Read, oh, master, read and smile!" He tossed the *Herald* on Chip's bed opened to the sports page.

STATE AND A. & M. MEET FOR CONFERENCE CHAMPIONSHIP

Game of The Week To Be Televised

BY BILL BELL

State and A. & M. meet for the conference championship Thursday afternoon in the game of the week which will be televised over a national hook-up and watched by more than twenty-five million fans. The defending champion, A. & M., is a strong favorite with practically every writer in the country, but this writer would like to go on the record as a challenger of the consensus.

The defending champion, A. & M., has a far better record. However, this is a game in which records and every other advantage, fact and fancy, goes overboard when the teams line up to do battle.

Your old standby will be covering his forty-third game between these two rivals and feels he has been around long enough to know what he is writing about. Therefore, in this story and on these pages, as witness, he goes right out on the proverbial limb and selects State as the team which will sport the conference crown when the sun sets on the Aggie Stadium Thursday afternoon.

Not the least of the factors which influence this reporter is the presence in the State line-up and in good health of State's "Mister Toe," Chip Hilton, who can do everything with a football except make it talk. . . .

Chip tossed the paper on the floor. "Why does he do that!" he said irritably. "Every game! I don't see why the rest of the team don't get up a petition to 'stop the Hilton publicity'!"

"Perhaps it's because they feel the same way," Soapy said. "You know something, Chipper. If the squad held a meeting to decide the most popular man on the team, you'd get every vote."

"Oh, stop it, Soapy," Chip said angrily. "You're as bad as Bill Bell! He doesn't know what he's talking about half the time. Why doesn't he write about the team? Teams win games, not individuals."

"He does," Soapy said. "Read on! Read it out loud."

Chip picked up the paper from the floor and continued, reading aloud. " 'Hilton runs like Red Grange, passes like a Sid Luckman, handles the ball like another Houdini, blocks and tackles with the best of them, and can play sixty minutes of knock 'em down and drag 'em out football. But it's his kicking which gives State the edge. Hilton's punting average is one of the best in the country. And his deadly field-goal accuracy will be a three-point threat every time State is stopped inside the Aggie thirty-yard line.

" 'Further, this prognosticator feels that in good old dependable Mike Brennan, Ace Gibbons, Tiny Tim McCarthy, and Larry Higgins, State has four veterans who could replace their respective A. & M. opponents with plenty to spare.

" 'A. & M. is loaded with veterans but the record proves that Curly Ralston knew what he was doing when he benched State's regulars of last year and risked his reputation on seven newcomers—Biggie Cohen, Philip Whittemore, Soapy Smith, Joe Maxim, Speed Morris, Fireball Finley, and Chip Hilton.'

"Now that's more like it," Chip said. "Hey! He picked you over Dex Clark! Shows he knows his football!"

"But you just said—"

"Never mind! I take it back!"

"O.K. Now read what Jim Locke says!"

STATE BURIES WESLEYAN 40–14

Ministers No Match For Cocksure Statesmen

By Jim Locke

University, *Nov. 21.*—State ran roughshod over a weak Wesleyan team here today to win its seventh straight conference game and will meet A. & M. Thanksgiving Day in a bid for conference honors.

Both teams have played the Dukes. State was lucky to get by with a scoreless tie, while A. & M. trounced the Iron Men on November 13 by a score of 21 to 7.

A. & M. did not play today and will be well rested for the game on Thursday. This reporter has seen both teams in action and believes A. & M. will run State right out of the Aggie Stadium. The veteran Farmers pack too much experience for an overgrown bunch of freshmen and are headed for the National championship. Despite the presence of such stellar performers as Captain Mike Brennan, Ace Gibbons, Tiny Tim McCarthy, Dex Clark, and Larry Higgins, the game should end in a rout.

Curly Ralston has used his veterans sparingly this season with the exception of the five named above and has managed (with luck) to squeeze through a weak conference schedule and qualify for title consideration. The season schedules and results are shown below:

WHAT DO YOU THINK?

A. & M.		State	
30—Southwestern	13	24—Tech	21
28—Wesleyan	0	17—Brandon	14
51—Carlton	0	31—Carlton	6
28—Tech	2	29—Southwestern	27
33—Brandon	6	31—Cathedral	14
20—Midwestern	7	0—Dukes	0
39—Riordon	6	17—Midwestern	14
45—Cathedral	0	40—Wesleyan	14
21—Dukes	7		
295	41	189	110

"Likes us, doesn't he?" Chip said, smiling.

Soapy glowered. "'Overgrown bunch of freshmen,'" he growled. "Where does he get that stuff?"

The redhead was restless and went for a walk shortly afterward, while Chip hit the books. Soapy came back after lunch and brought Chip two sandwiches and a carton of milk. Then, at two o'clock, Mark called Chip on the telephone.

"Hi, Chip, this is Mark. We just finished the papers. You know something! Bucky followed us this morning and told Eddie that Rip and Skids had assigned him to check up on Eddie until they got back. They said Rip and Skids were going to give me a going over unless Eddie showed up for the meeting Tuesday night."

"What's Eddie going to do?"

"I don't know, Chip. But he'd be mad if he knew I called you."

"I won't tell him. But you be sure to call me if Eddie ever goes down in that alley with Rip or Skids. O.K.?"

"Sure, Chip. Sure."

"All right. See you tomorrow night."

Thanks to the school vacation, Ralston called practice for two o'clock on Monday afternoon and kept them at it until six o'clock. Eddie showed up that evening still showing signs of his battle with Bucky Husta, but he was back in his shell and Chip said nothing about the game or the tickets. It was the same on Tuesday. Eddie wouldn't speak except to answer a direct question, and Chip let him stew it out.

Mark dropped in for his malted around eight o'clock and could barely conceal his excitement. Chip recognized the signs and sent Eddie on an errand. Mark started talking as soon as Eddie was out the door. "Rip and Skids are back, Chip. They got back this afternoon and Tony said they were going to hold the meeting tonight."

"Let them hold it," Chip said lightly. "I'm not interested unless Eddie joins them. Here's a dime. Now you go home and call me right away if Eddie goes to that meeting. You remember the number at Jeff?"

Mark nodded. "I have it, Chip." He walked slowly to the door and hesitated. Then he turned. "Chip," he said in a low voice, "you know something! I'm scared!"

CHAPTER 19

NEIGHBORHOOD AWAKENED

EDDIE REDDING raised himself cautiously on one elbow and looked intently at his brother. Then, satisfied that the little fellow was asleep, Eddie slipped out of the bed and dressed quickly and silently. Holding his shoes in one hand he crept to the door, opened it a crack and listened. Hearing no sound in the house, he descended the steps to the first floor and quietly slipped out the front door.

Upstairs, at the window fronting on the street, Mark watched Eddie walk west toward the candy store. Then Mark pulled on his shirt and trousers, made sure that the dime for the telephone call was still in his pocket, and put on his sneakers. He moved down the steps like a shadow and disappeared east in the direction of Main Street.

Chip was just dozing off when he heard the ringing of the telephone. He glanced at the alarm clock and then at Soapy. It was eleven-thirty and his pal appeared sound asleep. Before Pete Randolph could reach his apartment door, Chip was at the telephone. It was Mark.

"You better hurry, Chip. Eddie just went up the street."

"Where are you?"

"At a cigar store on Main Street."

"All right. Now, pay attention. You go right home and stay there. I'll have Eddie back there in no time. Right?"

"Right, Chip. But be careful."

Chip hurried upstairs and dressed quietly. Then he tiptoed out of the room, down the steps, and out the front door. His long legs carried him swiftly and silently along the quiet streets. As he ran, he tried to plan his campaign. But everything was so uncertain that he decided to let matters take their own course.

Soapy awakened just as Chip went down the steps. And he heard the front door close. He got up abruptly and quickly awakened Chip's pals and told them to get up and dress. "Meet me in my room," he whispered. "Right away!"

They were right on his heels in various stages of attire. "Chip's in trouble," he said bluntly.

"What do you mean?" Biggie asked. "How do you know?"

"I just know," Soapy said. "Eddie Redding is in trouble with some toughs and Chip's gone to help."

"At this time of night?" Whittemore said incredulously. "Why, it's twenty minutes to twelve."

"That's why I know it's trouble," Soapy said shortly. "Chip wouldn't break training rules unless it was serious."

"You know where he went?" Biggie demanded.

"I've got a good idea."

"Well, what are we waiting for?" Fireball said,

starting for the door. "If Chip's in trouble, I want a piece of it! Training rules or no training rules!"

Biggie Cohen suddenly filled the door. "Now wait a minute," he said quickly. "I'll go with Soapy and the rest of you stay here and stay out of trouble. We won't need any help."

"Maybe not," Fireball said crisply, "but you're going to have it! If it comes to a choice between training rules and helping Chip, I'm on my way!"

Whittemore nodded emphatically. "Me, too!" he said. "Let's go!"

Schwartz suddenly erupted into action, dashing for the door and ducking under Biggie's heavy arm. "Hold it a minute," he cried over his shoulder. "Gotta get my shoes!"

Meanwhile, Chip had reached and ducked into the same doorway in which he and Mark had waited the night of the truck incident. There was a crowd on the corner. Right in the middle of the group, he could make out Eddie and Tony and Rip and Skids. Rip had Eddie by the shirt collar and was shaking him and yelling in his face. Tony was listening impassively, his arms folded across his chest.

Chip stepped boldly out on the sidewalk and started across the street. Eddie was the first to see him and tried to push Rip's hand away. Rip turned then and saw the advancing figure. His grip on Eddie's collar loosened. He was shocked for a brief moment but recovered his swaggering assurance when Skids moved beside him.

"Well, well," he said mockingly. "Look who's here! The social worker!"

Chip kept on going until he was right in front of the fellow. "That's right," he said easily. "The social worker! I got to thinking about the tickets and what you said about making something out of it and I figured this was as good a time as any—"

"So what?" Rip sneered. "Go ahead! Make something out of it!"

The boys had pressed closely about Rip and Chip at first, but now they began to move back in awed silence, hardly grasping what it was all about. Chip saw Tony move closer to Skids, and Eddie began to edge toward Bucky. This was getting out of hand. A gang fight would do more harm than good. He would have to act fast.

He stepped back, thrilled by the knowledge that Tony was won over and ready to side with him if a fight was necessary. "I understand that you're a pretty good boxer," he said coolly. "How about you and me settling this with gloves? Down at the Y or the PAL? That's a pretty good way to settle differences if they can't be ironed out intelligently. In a fair fight with gloves."

Rip laughed boisterously. "Now ain't that just like a social worker. We're s'posed to settle all this with a coupla pillows laced clear up to our elbows. What d'ya know about that, Skids!" His voice hardened. "Why up at the Y, social worker? Why not down in the alley? Why not right now?"

"With gloves?"

"Sure! Sure, with gloves!" Rip cast an exaggerated wink in Skids' direction. "Go over to Moran's house, Skids, and get the gloves. You know, the real ones—" He laughed sarcastically. "We gotta fight fair, ya know!"

The crowd of boys suddenly broke for the alley, each anxious to get a good position. Eddie and Tony moved over and walked silently along beside Chip as he sauntered down toward the alley. Up ahead, Rip and Bucky and several small admirers swaggered along.

Frank Caruso had heard the argument on the corner and had been surprised to see Chip. But he knew trouble when he saw it, and instead of interrupting, he left the store unattended and hurried across the street to get Tony's father. Standing unconcernedly in the same doorway in which Chip had paused was a formidable group of athletes who were watching the proceedings with more than cursory interest. Fireball and Whitty were all for barging in and breaking it up fast, but Biggie checked them.

"Hold it!" Biggie commanded. "This is something personal. Chip wants it this way or he'd have let us know. Now you hold it, Fireball, Whitty. Chip can take care of himself. We'll move in if they gang up on him."

"That's right," Soapy agreed nervously. "Hold it."

"But we can't stand here and let him get beat up by a bunch of toughs," Fireball growled.

"They're not all toughs," Soapy protested. "Some of those kids are all right. Besides, Chip says half of these gang fights start because fellows with yellow streaks need a crowd behind them before they'll fight."

"Well, he's sure sticking to his principles," Schwartz said. "Now, where are they going?"

"We'll find out," Biggie said. "Come on. Easy now. Don't make any noise."

With Biggie leading the way, they kept in the shadows of the buildings and gained a position in the alley across the street without being seen. From this vantage point they could see Chip and Eddie, backed up against Caruso's garage, facing Rip and

Bucky and the rest of the group who were lined up along the high board fence.

"Some odds," Speed whispered hoarsely. "What in the world is it all about?"

Part of Speed's question was answered right then, for Skids appeared out of the dark street and tossed a pair of boxing gloves disdainfully at Chip's feet. Then Skids began to lace the other pair on Rip's hands.

Tony and Bucky and Eddie and others in that group had played many a game of marbles "for keeps" in that alley, but no game and no argument had ever been quite so important as this one.

Brisk footsteps sounded down the narrow street and Frank Caruso and Tony's father appeared. "Whatsa trouble here?" Caruso demanded. "Mr. Chip, you O.K.?"

"I'm all right, Mr. Caruso. Rip Grasco and I are settling a little argument with boxing gloves."

"Not with those gloves," Caruso said, snatching one from Skids' hands. "Tony tell me about this gloves! Looka this! Looka this lead!"

Chip examined the glove. Sure enough, a short length of lead as thick as a broom handle had been sewn on the inside of the glove. "Real clever, Rip," he said. "Real fair, too. A fair fight with gloves. Only your pair is loaded with lead weights!"

"You asked for it, sucker," Rip snarled. "What are you cryin' about?"

"I'm not crying. We'll settle this fifty-fifty. You take one and I'll take the other. O.K.? Your choice."

Rip snorted gleefully. "I'll keep the one I got on," he said, banging his gloved right hand against the fence."

Frank Caruso helped Chip lace on his gloves. "You sure you wanta fight, Mr. Chip? You want I should call Pop King?"

Chip shook his head. "No, Mr. Caruso, I'd rather settle it this way. I think we can settle a lot of things tonight."

"You said it, social worker," Skids said. "You're gonna settle right down on your back for a nice long sleep. Real soon now!"

The boys lined up along the fence snickered at the quip, but the face of young Tony Carlara remained serious, his expression unchanged. The sturdy youngster hadn't said a word since Chip had joined the group on the corner. But Chip noticed that Tony was now surrounded by most of the kids in the group. A few others were standing further along the fence beside Bucky.

Something new had been added across the street in the alley. Pop King had appeared from nowhere, it seemed, startling everyone except Fireball and Soapy.

"Boy, am I glad to see you!" Soapy whispered. "You gonna break it up?"

"No," King drawled. "I don't think so. We'll just see what happens."

The gloves were on now, and Chip advanced toward Rip and held out his gloved hands, palms down, in the traditional gesture of readiness. But Chip was facing a dirty fighter. Rip faked the touch and swung hard for Chip's jaw with the weighted right glove. But the glove merely whistled through the air as Chip drew back and instinctively stepped forward again with a hard left hook. The blow cracked flush against Rip's jaw, a square, jarring

"Chip drew back and instinctively stepped forward again with a hard left hook."

blow which thudded dully and half paralyzed the snarling roughneck. Rip groaned and fell forward to his knees.

It had been a terrific shot with the loaded glove, and the fight ended right there as far as Rip was concerned. Chip turned away and held out his hands so the laces could be untied. Caruso went to work on one and Eddie eagerly began on the other.

"You never lead with a right, eh, Chip?" Eddie chuckled.

Then it happened. Skids leaped behind Chip and struck him over the head with a short club. Chip tumbled forward as Rip gained his feet. Half-dazed, Chip fell to his knees, and saw Rip and Skids and Bucky tear into Frank Caruso and Eddie Redding.

"We'll teach you to stick your nose in our business," Rip rasped, raining blows on Caruso and knocking him to the ground. Skids grabbed Eddie and banged his head against the garage door and Bucky and Rip turned on Tony Carlara's father. The little man didn't have a chance against the two boys and Rip knocked him to the ground.

"There!" Rip panted viciously. "I guess you know who's boss around here now!"

Chip was struggling to get back on his feet, his head swimming and his thoughts reeling. He'd lost his big chance. Just when he had the whole thing whipped. . . .

In the alley on the other side of the street Soapy was struggling with Pop King. "Wait fellows," King said sharply. "Hold it!"

"But aren't you going to stop it?" Soapy demanded. "They haven't got a chance!"

"Just sit tight, sonny," King said. "There's more at stake than a couple of black eyes. Hilton can take care of himself, and unless I'm a rookie, this whole neighborhood is just about to wake up and get organized. Now watch!"

Chip had his senses back now and sprang to his feet. There was still a chance. . . .

He rushed to help Caruso and Carlara just as Rip, Skids, and Bucky turned around. This time, Chip had help. Young Tony Caruso flashed past him like a panther and landed all over Skids Welks. And Mark Redding was right behind, tearing into Bucky Husta like a raging fox terrier.

That left Rip. But before Chip could move, John Redding, still grimy from work, was on top of the bewildered ruffian, landing lefts and rights and knocking him to the ground before he had a chance to get his breath. Chip turned to help Mark and Tony, but it was all over. Skids was cowering on the ground with Tony standing over him, and Eddie and Mark were holding a cringing Bucky against the garage door.

So, just like that, it was all over. As Pop King had said, a whole neighborhood had awakened and joined forces and become organized.

King led the way, and as Chip's pals reached the scene, they heard Rip Grasco pleading with the bunch of bewildered kids who still lined the fence for help.

"C'mon, you guys," Rip pleaded in a hysterical voice. "C'mon, help us! Gang 'em!"

"You better help!" Skids threatened.

But Rip and Skids had been humilated. They had lost the fight and their leadership, and the kids turned them down flat. Right then, Biggie gave the whole crowd of youngsters the greatest kick they would ever have—gave them something to talk about for months to come. Biggie winked at Pop King and said, "O.K., I'll help you, fellow!"

Then he lifted Rip up in his arms and tossed him clear over the fence. Not to be outdone, Fireball grabbed Skids and threw him even higher and further. Then he swooped down on Bucky. "How about this one?" he cried.

Young Tony Carlara shook his head. "Never mind him," he said firmly. "I can handle him from now on." He shoved Eddie and Mark aside and jerked Bucky to his feet. "Right?" he demanded.

"Right, Tony," Bucky said. "Right!"

The kids had doubled over with laughter at the sight of Rip and Skids sailing over the fence, but there was also a great deal of awe in their faces. Then, as Biggie and Fireball and Whitty and Soapy and Speed and Red crowded around Chip, the kids recognized the invaders.

"I know you!" one boy cried, tugging at Biggie's arm. "You're Biggie Cohen! No wonder you could throw Rip over the fence. You must weigh three hundred!"

"Yeah, and the other guy's Fireball Finley!" another cried. "The fullback!"

Frank Caruso made the move which broke up the affair. "Come on," he cried, grabbing Chip by the arm. "We all go to my friend Tony's house. Come on, Mr. Redding you come too! Come on you footballs, we have some wine!"

Soapy started to explain that they were not allowed to drink wine and that they were in training and then stopped in the middle of the sentence. "Hey," he cried, "come on! It's after midnight! We're in trouble. We gotta run for it!"

"I've got to go, too," Chip told Caruso and Carlara.

"But we're going to organize a club for the kids," Mr. Carlara, protested. "Mr. Redding and Frank and me and Pop King and—"

"Yeah," Caruso interrupted, "and we're going to call him the Mr. Chip Club!"

Chip promised to be back the next day, and he and his pals sprinted up Tenth Street for all they were worth.

"If someone sees us now—" Soapy breathed.

At Tenth and Main, a string of cars from both directions were halted for the red light. Chip's crowd breathed a sigh and made a dash for it. Half-way across, Soapy stopped dead in his tracks, completely demoralized. "Oh, no!" he moaned. "Look! The coach's car! It's the coach!"

CHAPTER 20

SOPHOMORE SOMNAMBULISTS

HENRY ROCKWELL couldn't believe his eyes. "It can't be," he said incredulously. "Chip and Soapy and Biggie and Speed and Red and—why, almost every sophomore on the squad! It's just impossible!"

"Where in the world could they have been?" Sullivan asked. When neither of his companions replied, he muttered half-aloud, "Now what?"

Each of the three coaches was thinking of the men who had accompanied them to Cleveland and who had been in the car behind them when they stopped for the red light at Main and Tenth. The head coach was the one to break the silence.

"Nothing else to do," Ralston muttered. "Got to do it! Well, let's get it over." He braked the car to a stop and led the way into the Campus Restaurant and to a booth in the corner. Bill Bell and Jim Locke were right on his heels, smelling a story and anxious to be in on the ground floor. "Did you see—" Locke began.

"Yes, I saw," Ralston said calmly, "but I don't know any more about it than you do."

"Curfew in effect?" Bell asked.

Ralston nodded. "Yes," he said slowly. "Eleven o'clock."

"Sure caught them red-handed," Locke said slyly. "Any comment?"

Ralston chewed at his lower lip and thought it over. "No," he said shortly, "I guess not."

"But they're ineligible as of now," Locke persisted.

"Yes," Ralston said, "until I get a reasonable explanation."

"What's reasonable?" Locke demanded.

Ralston rose abruptly. "That I can't answer right now," he said coolly. "I guess I won't wait for coffee. Good night."

"But what about a statement?" Locke persisted. "What—"

But Ralston was gone, leaving the group to speculate and form their own opinions. Rockwell and Sullivan were tight-mouthed and would make no comment. Soon the group split up, confused and disturbed in varying degrees.

Locke broke the story with a headline in the *News* that morning, filling his column with suppositions and nasty speculations with respect to the "red-handed apprehension." He went on to state in his opinion that "the suspension of the sophomore somnambulists might be a blessing in disguise, since Ralston will now be forced to rely on his veterans and that will give State an outside chance for an upset."

Soapy got an early copy of the paper and brought it back to substantiate his dire forebodings. At nine o'clock Chip and his pals met to decide the proper course of action. While they were talking, Soapy again scurried out to get sandwiches and coffee.

"Good thing we're on vacation," he reported when he returned. "We'd probably be run off the campus. It's all over town! Only thing people are talking about! What're we gonna do?"

"*We* are not going to do anything," Chip said pointedly. "It was my personal project and *I'm* going to report to Ralston and assume the responsibility. It was my fault and mine alone."

"That's not true," Cohen said gently. "None of us *had* to go, Chip. We went because we *wanted* to go. There's a big difference."

Try as he might, Chip could not shake his pals on that point, and they were right behind him when he reported to Coach Ralston's office at ten o'clock. The head coach and his two assistants were waiting when the players filed into the office.

Chip got right to the point. "I guess you know why we're here, Coach," he said. "I'd like to explain first, sir, that the rest of the fellows were only trying to help me out of a difficulty."

"That's not quite correct, Coach," Biggie corrected. "We all knew exactly what we were doing and we're as much responsible as Chip."

"Just what is it all about?" Ralston asked.

"It's a personal matter, sir," Chip said. "The rest of the fellows thought that I might get into trouble."

"What sort of a personal matter?"

"It's hard to explain, sir. It was something I didn't have to do and still had to do— It's rather mixed up, sir."

"But you don't seem to understand. I *have* to have some sort of an explanation. Otherwise, you leave me no alternative. I'll be forced to suspend the whole group."

"But I'm the only one concerned, sir."

"And you won't disclose the reason for breaking the curfew?"

"I'd rather not, sir."

Ralston shook his head. "I don't understand it." He turned to the others. "How about you fellows? Any explanation to make?"

There was no answer. Ralston sighed and rose slowly to his feet. "Then you force me to drop all of you from the squad," he said, turning wearily away. "That's all."

"Now what do we do?" Soapy asked when they reached the street.

"I know what I'm going to do," Chip said disconsolately. "I'm going home."

"Valley Falls?" Soapy said incredulously. "And face your mother and all your friends? Not me!"

"That's up to you," Chip said. "But that's where I'm going."

"When do we leave?" Soapy said in a subdued voice.

Chip turned to Fireball and Whitty. "Mother was expecting us Thursday night after the game," he said, smiling regretfully. "I guess it's all right if we show up a little early. That is, if you still want to go."

"We wouldn't go anywhere else," Whitty and Fireball chorused. "Let's go!"

"All right!" Speed barked. "I'll get the limousine."

Thirty minutes later they were on their way, seven husky athletes all jammed in Speed's red-trimmed jalopy. And six hours later they pulled up before Chip's house, muscles cramped, badly shaken up, and spirits low.

The light was burning on the Hilton front porch. When she heard Speed's klaxon, Mary Hilton rushed out the door, down the steps, and out on the sidewalk. Chip kissed her and soon they were all seated in the kitchen enjoying big pieces of chocolate cake and mugs of milk.

"What happened, Chip?" Mary Hilton asked. "All I could get on the radio was something about you and the boys being suspended for breaking training rules."

Chip told his mother the story from beginning to end while his buddies listened. "So that's it, Mother," he said, when he finished. "There wasn't much of a choice."

"You did just right," his mother said. "I'm proud of you. But couldn't you tell the coach what you've told me? Wouldn't he understand?"

Chip nodded. "He'd understand, all right, Mother. But a fellow can't ask for sympathy or take credit for helping a friend. I just couldn't do it. It would sound like trying to be a hero or something like that. I don't care for myself, but it isn't right for the rest of the fellows to suffer just because they wanted to help *me*."

"You wanted to help Eddie, didn't you?" Biggie said softly. "You wanted to prove you were his friend. Well, we're no different, Chip. We wanted to help you and we wanted to prove our friendship just like you wanted to prove your friendship for Eddie."

Soapy changed the subject. "Bet the rest of the team would like to see us now," he chortled, snaring another big piece of cake. "Training is O.K., but you can't beat the simple pleasures of life."

Back in University, Frank Caruso was struggling with Bill Bell's story in the *Herald,* while Eddie and Mark and Tony and Bucky and the rest of the kids listened in mournful silence.

STATE STARS INELIGIBLE FOR CHAMPIONSHIP GAME

State Loses Seven Sophomore Stars For Training Irregularities

By Bill Bell

Chip "Mister Toe" Hilton, Biggie Cohen, Soapy Smith, Philip Whittemore, Red Schwartz, Speed Morris, and Fireball Finley are suspended for training violations.

Coach Curly Ralston announced today that seven of State's varsity players had been suspended for infraction of training rules. The seven players failed to observe the eleven-o'clock curfew rule which has been in effect all season. It is the second offense for Chip Hilton, who was benched for the game with the Dukes as a penalty.

Coach Ralston had journeyed to Cleveland last evening to attend a coach's meeting and was returning by car with assistant coaches Henry Rockwell and Jim Sullivan late last night. At the corner of Main and Tenth streets, the car bearing Ralston stopped for a red light and, at that precise moment, the seven players crossed the street. It was then 12:30 A.M.

The players reported to Ralston's office this morning, and when no satisfactory explanation was forthcoming, Ralston suspended the players.

Coach Ralston said he regretted the necessity for the action but that discipline and sportsmanship are as important in football as in everyday life and that a player who breaks training rules without an exceptional excuse has betrayed a trust and must be disciplined for the good of the game and his teammates.

State departed for Archton on the 11:40 this morning and will work out late this afternoon on the A. & M. freshman practice field. . . .

As soon as Frank Caruso finished reading the paper, Mark leaped to his feet. "You gotta do something, Eddie," he pleaded earnestly. "Chip and the whole bunch got in trouble on account of you."

"Me?"

"Yes, you! I told Chip about Rip and Skids gonna beat you up last night and that's why he showed up."

Eddie was shocked. "You mean you snitched!"

"Call it that if you want. Anyway, I told Chip and I told Pop when he came home from work. That's why Chip and Pop showed up."

"Now I get it," Eddie said. "I've been trying all day to figure out how come Chip and Soapy and Fireball and Whitty and all the football guys showed up. Sure we gotta do something! We gotta see the coach. We gotta see Ralston!"

"But he's gone," Tony said. "He left this morning with the team for Archton. Says that right in the paper."

"Then we gotta get to this Archton."

"What you going to use for money?" Tony asked. "Traveling on a train takes money."

Frank Caruso had been listening intently. Now he broke into the conversation. "You take the truck," he said excitedly. "Tony's brother Angelo, he can drive. Run, Tony! Tell your old man his friend Frank Caruso want to see him."

It was after midnight before the expedition was completely organized. But at last they were off, Angelo Carlara at the wheel of Caruso's truck, Mr. and Mrs. Carlara on the front seat beside him. In the back were John Redding, still dressed in his working clothes, Tony, Eddie, Mark, and Bucky.

Angelo Carlara triumphantly drove into Archton

at eight o'clock the next morning and sped down the main street just as if he knew where he was going. But he didn't, so it took the better part of an hour for them to locate Ralston and the team at the Hotel Western. Angelo parked right in front of the hotel and five minutes later had Ralston on the house telephone.

Ralston was bewildered by the garbled explanation but recognized the urgency in Carlara's voice and hurried down to the lobby. There he was immediately surrounded by the contingent, each member loudly trying to tell him the story.

While all this was going on in Archton, Chip and his pals were over on the high school field working out with the Valley Falls team. After a while, Chip borrowed a ball and they began to practice Tims Lansing's fake-kick play.

It was just nine-forty-five when Taps Browning, Chip's next-door neighbor, came dashing out on the field. Taps' long legs were flying. "Hey, Chip!" he yelled excitedly. "You hear the news? It's on radio and television and all over! You've been reinstated! The whole bunch! C'mon! You gotta hurry!"

Chip was bewildered. "What do you mean? How do you know?"

"Heard it on television not five minutes ago. Saw it myself! Seems a bunch of boys showed up in Archton and told the coach and the papers and everyone in town all about it.

"Another thing! Your mother's nearly frantic. Said Coach Rockwell had been burning up the wires trying to get you on the phone. C'mon! Hurry!"

"Hot dog!" Soapy yelled, tossing the football up in the air and sprinting for the jalopy. "C'mon, you guys! C'mon, Speed, get this junk pile movin'!"

The jalopy groaned with the added weight of the new passenger but it took off all right. On the way, Taps told how he had been watching a sports program from Archton. The broadcaster was interviewing the A. & M. coach when they broke it off and announced that Coach Ralston had reinstated his sophomores—except that he didn't know where they were—

"Then the broadcaster got about twenty kids on the screen and said they were friends of Chip Hilton and one of the boys told about you getting him out of trouble and then the broadcaster introduced the boy's father and mother and brother and three other boys and that's when I took off!"

Fireball elbowed Browning in the ribs and Taps winced. "You better not be kidding, bub," he said.

"On my honor."

The jalopy slid to a stop in front of the Hilton home and Chip hopped out. His mother was at work as supervisor of the local telephone exchange and must have been holding a wire open direct to the house, for she answered as soon as Chip put the receiver to his ear.

"Chip, did you hear the news? . . . Isn't it wonderful? You'll have to hurry! Start right away! I'll be looking for you home late tonight or tomorrow! Oh, yes. There's some money in the sideboard drawer under the silver box. Enough for gasoline and something to eat. It seems too good to be true, Chip, but it is! Henry Rockwell vouches for it. Henry says it all came about because of those boys you've been helping—

"Just a second now, Chip. Here he is, Henry. Go ahead, Chip."

Rockwell's relieved voice came loud and sharp and

excited through the receiver. "Chip! Everything's all right! Haven't got time to explain it now, but you've all been reinstated. Are the other fellows with you? . . . Good! You'll have to hurry. It's a long ride, clear across the state. Come right to the Aggie Stadium. Murph Kelly will have uniforms ready for you. Be careful now!"

Chip yanked the sideboard drawer open, grabbed the small roll of bills, and tore out of the house. "Lock the door, Taps!" he cried, diving headlong over the side of the car and right in the middle of the mass of bodies. "Let's go!" he yelled. "We're going to play!"

The jalopy grunted and roared and leaped away from the curb and Chip tried to answer all the questions. Thirty miles and thirty minutes later, Speed stopped for gas and Soapy wedged himself behind the wheel. "Been drivin' this baby carriage in low," he fumed. "Hold on to your toupees, you guys!"

"Better hold on to something," Fireball fumed. "Game's at two o'clock. It's eleven now, and we've got two hundred miles to go! Can't be done!"

"We can try," Chip said grimly.

Soapy tried all right, driving skilfully and carefully but fast. At twelve o'clock they pulled on to the thruway. The signs indicated they were 170 miles away from Archton, and Soapy really began to push the jalopy.

Chip was the first to see the police car on the side of the road. He tried to warn Soapy, but it was too late. Two state troopers stepped out in the road, flagged them down, and walked around beside Soapy.

"What's the hurry, young fellow?" the tall one drawled. "Going somewhere?"

"Er—sure," Soapy stammered. "What's the trouble, officers?"

"It's all yours, sonny. You realize that fifty miles an hour is the limit in this area?"

"Yes, sir! No, sir! That is—"

"Then why seventy miles an hour?"

"Seventy! Why this car couldn't do seventy down Mount Everest!"

"Here's the radar slip!"

"Radar slip?" Soapy gasped.

"That's right! Now get out of that contraption and let me have your driver's license."

Soapy got out of the car and began to search his pockets. "I guess I haven't got it," he said lamely.

"Seventy miles an hour, a driver without a license, and seven passengers in a car built for two! Hmm. Guess you'd better follow me."

"But we're football players!" Soapy cried. "We play for State! We gotta win the game!"

The other trooper grinned. "Oh, sure!" he said. "I'm the coach!"

CHAPTER 21

MOVE OVER, NOTRE DAME!

STATE TROOPERS are used to all sorts of excuses, alibis, apologies, and pleas. A good sense of humor is important in maintaining an even temperament for them. These particular troopers and the lieutenant in charge of their division were so blessed. When the troopers ushered the group through the door, the man at the desk looked up and smiled. "What's this—a football team?"

"That's what they say!" The first trooper said. "Claim to be on the State varsity and they say they're supposed to play against A. & M. this aft—"

"That's right!" Soapy interrupted. "We've got to get there! It's important! We've been reinstated!"

The eyes of the man at the desk became suddenly alert. "What's your name?" he snapped.

"Smith. Soapy Smith. And this is Chip Hilton and he's the regular State quarterback and—"

"Hold it! Could be, Tom— I heard something about it on the radio a little while ago. Where's that paper? Yesterdays *Herald* had the pictures of those players spread clear across the front page. Here it is!" He scanned the anxious faces. "Hmm. It's them all right.

"Well, now, that's different! Sit down! I've got to make a call." He jiggled the receiver. "Hello, hello! Clyde? . . . Get the captain at University. . . . Yes! Hurry, will you? It's important!"

Soapy grinned at the troopers and permitted himself the luxury of a deep sigh of relief. "You see," he said. "I told you!"

The man at the desk had reached his party. "Captain? . . . This is O'Brian. You know those State football players they've been looking for—well, they're right here in the office. I—" He listened, nodding his head from time to time. Then he glanced at the two troopers. "Tom Leeds and Bill Graham," he said. He listened again. "Yep, right here! . . . Yes, sir! Right away, sir! They're on their way!"

"All right, you two," he said briskly, addressing the troopers. "You're going to a football game. Captain's orders! Let's see. Twelve-thirty and one hundred and sixty miles. You'll never make the start of the game but you might make the last half if you're lucky. Captain said to get them there as fast as possible. Take two cars. Tom, you lead the way and keep in touch!

"Another thing, you," he said, addressing Soapy. "Park that refugee from a junk yard in the back out of sight. Good luck, you fellows. I'm a State rooter myself!"

Gloom was a foot thick in the State sections of the A. & M. oval. It was the end of the third quarter and right at the open end of the stadium, for every fan in the place to see, the reason for the depression of the State fans loomed in six-foot numerals: A. & M. 9, State 6.

The State veterans had put up a terrific fight in

the bitter battle but it had been apparent early in the first half that the guns to blast the tough A. & M. scoring zone were missing. But the State fans never gave up hope. They had been stimulated by the reports that Chip Hilton and the talented sophomores had been reinstated and would play, and they kept watching the State runway all afternoon.

A. & M. had scored on a touchdown and a safety, while State had capitalized on the recovery of an Aggie fumble on the ten-yard line in the third quarter for their only score. Ace Gibbons had punched his way across for the touchdown in four tries but had failed on the try for the extra point. That had been the last time State had gotten close to pay dirt.

Gee-Gee Gray was doing his best to encourage the State fans, and the television commentator was following suit. Back in University, in Frank Caruso's candy store, Pop King and half the neighborhood had been crowded around the set, ever since the startling and almost unbelievable news had spread through the area that the Carlara and Redding families and Bucky Husta had made their appearance on television that morning from Archton.

It was the same in State Drug and in the PAL Center on Main Street. Lieutenant Byrnes divided his time between the television set and his desk. And in Valley Falls, at the Sugar Bowl and in the headquarters of the Hilton Athletic Club, it was the same. Mary Hilton, home from work, had the television going in the living room and the radio blasting away in the kitchen. And Mrs. Browning and Taps and a whole slew of the kids who knew Chip and made his house their headquarters were parked before the set, watching and waiting for his appearance.

Troopers Tom Leeds and Bill Graham kept their

radios tuned to Gee-Gee Gray during the desperate race with time. Leeds used the siren when necessary to clear the road, but it was a tough assignment, and the game was in the fourth quarter when they braked to a sharp stop in front of the Aggie Stadium. The troopers left the cars right there in the entrance and led the way to State's dressing room, where Murph Kelly and his two assistants dressed Chip and the gang in nothing flat. Then the troopers led the mad dash out on the field.

Somehow, the fans had sensed the arrival of the players even before they dashed out the runway. The State troopers, Tom Leeds and Bill Graham got the biggest cheer they would ever hear, much less receive, when they sprinted through the runway with the sophomores.

State had the ball on their own thirty-yard line, second down and nine, with five minutes left to play, when Mike Brennan heard the thunderous roar and called for a time-out.

Chip took in the score, the position of the ball on the field, and the time left to play in one glance. Then Ralston grabbed him by the hand and nearly tore his arm out of the socket when he swung him right out on the field. The head coach did the same with the others and they tore out to report. The veterans gave them a welcome cheer and pounded them on the backs. Those they replaced trotted off the field leaving no doubt in anyone's mind how they felt about the kids.

Every person in the stadium was on his feet, the State fans cheering like maniacs and the Aggie rooters joining in the uproar because they were carried away by the dramatic impact of the moment.

The A. & M. players stood with hands on hips,

their expressions curious and appraising. "So the stars have arrived to win the game," one remarked sarcastically.

"You'll be seein' stars, buddy boy," Soapy retorted. "On the first play!"

Chip passed to Whittemore before the Aggies knew he had the ball, and Whitty went way up in the air to pull the toss down on the State forty-five. Then Fireball tore through the middle for twelve vital yards to put the ball on the A. & M. forty-three-yard line, and the Aggie captain called time.

When time was in, Chip sent Speed tearing through left tackle for four yards, passed again to Whittemore on a buttonhook which was good for seven and the first down, and the Aggie captain again called time. This time the A. & M. coach sent his big first line back in the game, to give the Aggie fans something to cheer about.

During the time-out, Chip studied the clock, the position of the ball, and the path to the goal line thirty-two yards away. Time for only a few more plays, he was thinking. What to do? What would Tims Lansing do in this situation?

The field judge waved and Chip called the play in the huddle. "Freeze it, Fireball!" he cautioned.

Finley took off on the quick-opening play like a jet plane but didn't gain an inch. The big Aggie line rose up like a stone wall and carried him back for five yards before he toppled to the ground and was buried under an avalanche of bodies. The Aggie fans cheered the play to the skies. Fireball took a long time getting up, shaking his head and holding his shoulder. The referee brought the ball back to the A. & M. thirty-two-yard line, squarely in the middle of the field, and Mike Brennan called time.

It was second down now, and Chip once again glanced at the clock. "Got to stay in the center of the field," he muttered.

In the huddle he called for a pass into the end zone. "Thirty-three X on two, gang," he said. Then he looked at Whittemore. "I'm going to throw it high, Whitty. Can't risk an interception."

Time was in then, and the roar from the stands came booming around Chip. "One, two, three—"

He faded back, faked to Speed in the flat, and barely got the ball away. But it was too high, sailed above Whittemore's hands and out of bounds behind the end zone.

Chip again glanced at the clock. "Thirty-one! Cross-buck, gang. All yours, Fireball. On three, gang, let's go!"

Chip faked to Gibbons, pivoted quickly, and gave Fireball the ball. But the Aggie middle-guard broke through and tackled Fireball just as he got the ball. Fireball fought his way back to the line and Chip cast a frantic glance at the clock and yelled, "Time!" Fourth and time for all or nothing at all . . . One last play! . . . Fourth down showdown! . . .

Chip looked at the scoreboard and studied the clock and the big numerals: A. & M. 9, State 6. Then he walked over behind the ball and sighted the line to the goal. Once more his thoughts turned to Tims Lansing. What would Tims do *now* if he were calling the plays? Would Tims try for the tie or for the win? . . .

"Tims would go all the way," Chip breathed to himself, "all the way! Wouldn't it be great if his play could win the game?" He sighted the line from the ball to the goal once more and then hustled back to the huddle. On the way he passed the referee and without looking at the man he whispered sibilantly, "Trick play coming up! Please watch!" Then he knelt in the center of the huddle. "Time for one last play, fellows. It's now or never—"

Mike Brennan slapped him on the back. "You can do it, Chipper. We'll hold 'em!"

"Say that again," Finley rasped. "You can kick this one blind-folded!"

Chip shook his head. "We're not kicking!" he whispered cautiously. "We're playing to win!"

The circle tightened as the import of the words struck home. "Now, listen," Chip said sharply. "We're going to use Tims Lansing's play, the fake-kick! Everyone know it?"

"*We* oughta know it," Soapy said. "We practiced it all morning."

"Speed can do it," Chip continued, "but he's got to have good blocking. Fireball's got to get the end, Biggie takes the tackle, and Whitty's got to flatten the right backer-up." He grabbed Mike Brennan by the arm. "That leaves the key block for you, Mike. You've got to get downfield and block the right halfback." He turned to Speed. "Be sure to have *both* knees *off* the ground when you catch the ball! Well, that's it! Go get 'em, gang!"

Chip and Mike clasped hands and the team joined in the grip. "This one is for Tims," Chip gritted. "On the count of three, gang! Let's go!"

Most football crowds start for the exits when there are only seconds to play. But these fans were different. The annual State–A. & M. game was the game of any week and any year for them. And this game today was one of the greatest of all time. They stood tense and immobile as State came out of the huddle and formed in place-kick alignment. The Aggie fans began to chant, "Block that kick!"

When Chip lined up the kick and dropped back, the chant grew to a tremendous roar. The rhythmic thunder of "Block that kick! Block that kick! Block that kick!" caught up the whole crowd. For a moment even the State fans were tempted to join in the chorus, although that would mean rooting against their own team.

The thundering roar seemed a greater obstacle to Chip than the players on the field. It seemed to build up a wall between the ball and the precious goal line thirty-two yards away. Thirty-two long, desperately long yards, plus ten more to clear the crossbar above the end-zone line. Chip concentrated on the strip of tape Speed had stretched toward the center of the crossbar; tried with every bit of his being to feel, to *know*, that he was going to kick the ball squarely between the uprights.

The ball came spinning back to Speed, true and fast, and the mighty roar from the stands seemed to lift the A. & M. forwards over and through the State line as if it were paper. The groan of anguish from the State fans almost equaled the home rooter's cheers as the big linemen charged toward Chip.

Chip stepped forward, concentrating on the ball for all he was worth, and kicked right through Speed's arms. Then he lifted his head and eyes as though watching the ball in flight. Just before the Aggie forwards hurled him to the ground, he heard a tremendous shout of dismay from the A. & M. rooters and turned his head just in time to glimpse Speed tearing around left end and heading for pay dirt only yards away.

The big linemen buried him under their massive bodies then, but he heard the exultant roar of the State fans. Chip never saw Speed cross the goal line and toss the ball to the field judge, just as the startled official pulled the trigger of the gun ending the game. But he knew the play he and his pals had practiced so carefully that morning in Valley Falls had worked; knew each and every one of them had performed his part perfectly.

Up in the broadcasting booth, Gee-Gee Gray gave a piercing shout into the mike just as Speed crossed the goal line and let the roar of the State fans tell the story to his listeners. And just a few feet away, Jim Locke grimaced and shouted, "Lucky! S'pose it hadn't worked?"

Bill Bell grinned and shouted back, "But it did! The kids were somnambulating when they worked that one out!"

Seconds later, Chip booted the ball smack through the middle of the uprights and turned in time to see the big numbers on the scoreboard shift as if by magic: A. & M. 9, State 13.

Chip knew there were sixty thousand spectators in the stadium, but he didn't know that thirty million other game-of-the-week televiewers saw his teammates hoist Speed and himself to their shoulders and carry them around and around the field.

High up in the concrete bowl, Mr. Carlara was holding a copy of the *Herald* in his hand and showing anyone who would look, the picture of Chip and his buddies. "That's my boy!" he shouted. "Tony and Angelo, here, they're my boys. But this one"—He poked his finger through Chip's picture— "This one! He's my boy, too!"

Chip would have enjoyed hearing Mr. Carlara say

that and would have liked to see the proud expressions on the faces of Eddie and Mark and Tony and John Redding and Bucky Husta. But right then, he was riding on a wave of shoulders, and back in the line of celebrants he could see Speed and Soapy and Captain Mike Brennan and Fireball and Whitty and Larry Higgins and Red Schwartz and Biggie Cohen and Ace Gibbons bouncing along like Arabs riding a string of camels.

Curly Ralston and Rock and Jim Sullivan were standing up on the bench waving and yelling, and a crew of radiomen were trying to get their attention. Then they saw Chip and fought their way through the crowd and the announcer held the mike up to him and shouted, "Here, Hilton, say something! Say anything! You couldn't say anything wrong, right now, if you tried. Say hello to your mother! Go on!"

Chip took the mike with the long trailing cord and said, "Hello, Mother, we made it!" Then he grinned self-consciously and said to himself, "As if she doesn't know!" Then he remembered the fake-kick play and said, "Hello, Tims! Hello, Tims Lansing! Your play won the game! Hello, Mr. Grayson! Hello, Mr. Caruso! Hello, Mitzi! Hello, Pop King!"

Then Soapy came bouncing along and the announcer gave him the mike. But all Soapy would say was, "Move over, Notre Dame! You got company!"